CHRONICLES OF ESHA 2

# BETRAYAL
## OF THE
# SWORD

## TABITHA DAY

ISBN (ePub) 978-0-473-72344-6

ISBN (Paperback) 978-0-473-72343-9

ISBN (Kindle) 978-0-473-72345-3

Cover designed by GetCovers

Powered by Atticus

For those who have strayed...
And those who returned.

# THE STORY SO FAR

## CROWNING OF THE SWORD, CHRONICLES OF ESHA 1

The day Ember escapes from her abusive relationship on Earth is the day she is abducted by Cole, a handsome, charming fae battling for the crown of the Kingdom of Swords against his brooding cousin Ashe.

Ember's every desire is granted as she adjusts to a life of luxury in the royal castle, but when she and Cole grow closer, their romantic relationship takes a dark and dangerous turn. Cole turns her into a shell of what she used to be, stealing her memories, and sapping her will. Ember realises that if Cole wins the tournament, both she and the kingdom are doomed. Once he plucks the pendant from the flaming tree, he will be king, with Ashe condemned to be his second, confined inside the pendant until death.

In a desperate attempt to flee, she steals the pendant for herself, thwarting Cole's ambitions to rule, and using its power to take her back home, safe where she belongs.

Or so she thinks ...

# CHAPTER 1

"I think we need to talk."

Ember's face was expressionless as she turned to confront Ashe, although her hands were trembling and her heart was hammering so hard she was sure he'd be able to hear it, that the whole art gallery would hear it. She cast a surreptitious glance around. The room was practically empty. There was no one close enough to rescue her—as if anyone could, even if they were. Ashe was a prince of fae, with power enough that he could level the room to dust with a wave of his hand if he chose. And right now, he looked as if he really, really wanted to.

"The kingdom requests your presence," he continued.

That sentence, spoken as though it was a command to be obeyed, straightened her spine. "And I decline that request."

He considered her for a moment and turned his gaze to the painting on the wall before them. "Nice picture."

"Thank you."

The painting showed the castle where she'd been held prisoner, the castle that was Ashe's home, a looming, towering fairytale nightmare of grey stone, turrets, and towers, surrounded by thick fog where half-concealed monsters lurked. No one had ever described the picture as *nice*. Disturbing, perhaps. Predatory. Secretive. Much like Ashe himself, now she came to think of it.

She observed him from under her lashes as he continued to study her painting. He was as gorgeous as ever, but he looked tired, his expression wary. She'd only ever seen him in his military uniform of black before, but now, in an effort to fit in with Earthly style, he had adapted it to a pair of black jeans, a black shirt and a long black coat that seemed to swirl about him like smoke. The two of them were a dead match, she thought, tucking her hands into the pockets of her black trousers with what she hoped was a nonchalant air. Like a pair of night-time assassins.

"I'm not coming back, Ashe. Your world is your problem. I have a life now." She unclipped the pendant from around her neck and held it out to him. "Take it."

The orange stone flickered as though a shadow were moving restlessly around inside. His eyes widened, and he flinched back as though she were proffering a live snake and not a piece of jewellery. "It doesn't work like that."

She held it out for a moment longer and then slipped it back around her neck. "Fine."

The gallery owner came bustling over, champagne slopping over the side of her dangerously full glass. "Darling, are you off?"

She kissed the air somewhere by Ember's cheek, her eyes widening as she took in Ashe, and then she simpered, actually simpered, as though she were a teenager meeting her favourite movie star in the flesh. Ashe gave her a lazy smile, and wine splattered the concrete floor.

"Yep, we're off. I'll call you later," Ember said, swiftly heading for the exit before she had to do any introductions, before she had to explain who—or what—Ashe was.

He was at the door, holding it open for her before she reached it, and she wondered if the gallery owner had noticed how quickly, how fluidly he moved, but then they were out on the street in the crisp, autumn air, her breath puffing out in steamy clouds.

"Well," she said. "It was nice to see you again, Ashe."

She made to move off, but a hand shot out and he gripped her elbow, dragging her toward him. She'd been taking self-defence classes, a mix of martial arts, three times a week. She'd learned several ways to disengage from an attack, but the scent of him washed over her and she couldn't move a muscle, couldn't help her eyes drifting closed as she inhaled the seductive scent of fae, the smell of wildflowers, spices and honey, a fragrance that permeated her dreams sometimes.

"I haven't finished with you yet."

"Yes, you have," she snapped, giving her head a little shake to clear it, and yanking her arm free. "You can't just appear out of nowhere. It's been three years. I told you, I have a *life* ..."

"Three years for you. Just a week for us. A very long week."

The gallery owner was staring at them open-mouthed through the glass window and Ember gave her a quick reassuring smile, before muttering, "Come on. Before she tries to get your autograph."

She moved off down the street, Ashe at her side, her mind spinning. She knew enough about Ashe to realise that he wasn't going to just vanish because she asked him to, and she sure as hell wasn't going to take him back to her little city apartment just a few streets away. So, she compromised and steered him toward the local café, all dim lighting and dark corners and tattooed wait-staff with silver bars and jewelled studs through their faces. A TV screen on the wall played indie music videos, and the music thumped through the room.

She shepherded him to a corner table and ordered two flat whites at the counter. The barista looked over at her table and did a double take as she saw Ashe, a lascivious smile creeping over her face. "Well done," she said with a wink.

Ember chose to ignore this and returned to the table, dropping into her chair with a decided lack of grace. Even in this dark corner, Ashe seemed to *glow*. Tall and muscular, he took up more than his fair share of space. The lines and planes of his face were carved in perfect symmetry, his dark hair tousled just so, his eyebrows brooding, and the mouth, even though down-turned in barely concealed anger, was still full and soft. In his own world, his skin would have appeared as if lit by rainbows beneath the surface, but here, he just looked dewy and healthy, as though he spent all day getting massages, eating organic baby vegetables laced with vitamins, and drinking natural spring water from the foothills of some perfectly triangular mountain. Almost everyone in the café was watching him, either surreptitiously from behind their coffee cups, or in blatant admiration. He wasn't looking at any of them, though. His attention was fully focused on Ember.

As she stuffed her wallet back in her bag, he said, "You've left us in a bit of a mess."

"I don't care."

"You should."

"It's not my problem."

"You cut your hair."

She blinked, touching her short pixie-cut self-consciously, before she whipped her hand back down again, nestling it in her lap. The first thing she'd done when she got to the city was to cut her hair off. New woman, new hair, and all that.

"Ashe, I'm not going back. Are you going to kill me?"

He leaned back in his chair. "No. Nobody is going to kill you. Right now, you hold the kingdom. But with every delay, your world will be impacted."

She scoffed at that. "You lot love to throw that it my face. The earth is heating because of crappy decisions made by crappy politicians. Not because the Kingdom of Swords can't decide on a ruler. Besides, there hasn't been an extreme weather event in … I don't know. Ages."

He raised an eyebrow. "The pendulum is swinging. It won't be long until it's in a worse condition than it was before." He crooked a finger and the TV screen flicked to a news channel showing wildfires out of season, swallowing swathes of Australia's native bush.

The barista glanced at the screen in confusion and jabbed at a remote. The screen flicked back to the music.

Ember rolled her eyes. "You could have made that up."

"I didn't. And that's just the start."

"How did you get here? I thought only you *and* Cole could tear the veil between our worlds." Cole. Even the feel of his name in her mouth was enough to send a shudder down her back. She'd been his plaything for far too long.

"Cole is … indisposed. The Adjudicator sent me."

As he said this, the server approached with their coffee. She looked nervous as she set Ashe's cup in front of him, but he didn't even acknowledge her. Ember murmured thanks, trying to calm herself at the involuntary reaction she had at the mention of the Adjudicator. He was cold, terrifying, and he scared the shit out of Ember. "That's not good. For you."

Ashe scowled at her. The table rumbled ominously, making the coffee cups rattle in their saucers, and Ember couldn't help shooting a quick look at the door, wondering how far she would get before he blasted her into oblivion. "The Adjudicator runs the kingdom now. Until you come back and sort it out, we're fucked. We need a Sword."

"Then take the stupid pendant!" Ember hissed. "I only took it so I could use its power to get home. Neither you nor Cole were going to help me. I had to take matters into my own hands."

"I would have sent you home."

"But you didn't win. Cole did. And he's a monster." She picked up her cup and took a sip of her coffee.

Ashe did the same, his mouth twisting at the bitter taste. "That's awful."

She took an even bigger swallow just to spite him and set her cup down. "If I go back, Cole will kill me."

"If I can extract a promise from the Adjudicator that none shall harm you, will you consider it?"

She gave him a brief, wintry smile. "The thing is, Ashe, you can promise all the pretty things you like, but I'll never trust you or any other fae as long as I live."

She pushed her chair back and stood, grabbing her bag and coat.

He remained seated, his eyes hard. "So, not very long, then?"

She ignored that and strode out of the café, but she couldn't help glancing back through the window as she passed.

His chair was empty. He'd already vanished.

# Chapter 2

E mber scurried home, her pace growing faster and faster until she was practically running the last few metres before her front door. She tore up the steps, jabbing her key at the lock, cursing as the key skittered left and right before finally plunging home. Once inside, she made herself take a deep breath and then another before she calmly closed the door. Control, she reminded herself. You're in control.

She kicked off her shoes, flipped on the lights and bustled about, throwing her coat over the arm of the sofa, lighting a scented candle, pouring a glass of wine. Heat and music turned on automatically, and within a few minutes, the space was warm and welcoming. It was a rented apartment with cramped rooms, but the reason she'd chosen it was because of the loft space upstairs. The owner had told her the loft had always been used for storage, but Ember had paid little attention to the dust and cobwebs. She was too busy admiring the skylights and sash windows that let the light stream in on even the gloomiest of days. With an intense clean and a lick of white paint, it made a more than adequate painting studio. Her canvasses lined the walls, all of them dark and moody, the perfect contrast.

She'd tried to trick herself with the familiarity of an everyday routine, but it wasn't really working. Her heart was still pounding, and she could still feel him about her, his scent clinging to her clothes and hair, the aroma of red wine and vanilla candle doing little to combat the sweet smell of fae.

She spent a long time in the shower, washing her hair twice and covering herself in suds, and when she finally emerged, pink and glowing, she'd almost convinced herself that she had forgotten all about Ashe.

She walked back into the lounge, intending to go through her bag and look for a business card that a prospective client had left her, and started. She wasn't alone. Ember backed up, and then whirled and ran for the door, but a barrier closed over the door frame like an invisible skin, throwing her back onto the floor.

"Now, now, Miss Bailey," came an excruciatingly familiar voice, like that of a whispering breeze through winter boughs. "Let's not be hasty."

"I told Ashe I wasn't coming." She fumbled for the clasp of the pendant with trembling fingers. "I have it, you can take it, I tried to give it to Ashe ..."

The Adjudicator raised a withered hand, and she froze. Red pupils and clouded irises bore into her, drying up the words in her mouth. He considered her, head cocked to one side, and then she felt a tearing in her breastbone as though someone had driven a crowbar into her and was wrenching her bones apart.

She rolled onto her back, crying out in agony, hands clawing at the thing that was splitting her apart, but there was nothing there. She arched her back and gagged, fighting for air, fighting to get away. The pain abruptly stopped, and she gasped, tears streaming down her face. She crawled back as fast as she could, but there was nowhere to go. Back against the wall, she whimpered, a shaking hand outstretched as if to ward off the pain she knew was coming. And when it did, she cried out, clinging to the sound, letting it fill her and surround her and carry her away. And in that moment, the pain lessened enough for her to gather her wits.

Ashe had summoned the Adjudicator. The only reason the Adjudicator was here was to make a deal. Which meant she had the upper hand.

She almost laughed at that. Here she was, writhing and screaming on the floor, unable to get away, but she had the power. She'd offered him the pendant, and yet he'd made no move to take it. He was just torturing her because she had shamed him in front of the kingdom. He was torturing her because he could.

With a terrible effort, she fought against the pain, managing to raise her head high enough to lock eyes with him. "Stop it," she hissed.

Surprise filled into those horrible eyes, and he looked almost amused. "Very well."

The pain ceased. She lay on the floor recovering her breath, before getting slowly to her feet. The towel had slipped from her head and her robe had come untied, but she didn't think the Adjudicator had any interest in whether or not she was naked and she didn't bother readjusting it.

"Take the pendant." Her voice was shaking. "Take it and go. Cole won. He can rule. I don't care."

"It's not as simple as that," the Adjudicator said. "You ruined the tournament and they will have to fight for it again. The kingdom must have a Sword. The Treaty of Swords cannot be broken."

Ember blinked. She'd already witnessed three games of the tournament, had watched competing fae tear each other apart and die screaming. "Again?"

"Your fault," he told her, and like an echo in her mind, she heard those words spoken in another time, another place, and felt herself wither. "Earth may have had a brief respite from the heat, but the influence of the kingdom is taking effect. On the other side of the world, fires have already started. People will die. And that's on you."

She attempted to control her expression, although she could feel her lower lip beginning to tremble.

"You can't put climate change on me," she said, in as scathing a tone as she could muster.

"Humans. Always refusing to take responsibility." He sighed and then gave a thin-lipped smile that showed jagged, yellow teeth. He moved closer to her, and she could feel a chill emanate from him, as though someone had thrown the window open. "I can cause you pain upon pain upon pain. I can stop your heart with a squeeze of my hand and then start it again. I can make you beg for death. And when you do, when you are crying for me to kill you, I will not."

"I can't go back," she said, her voice pleading, although she knew the Adjudicator didn't have a whit of empathy in him. "Cole will kill me. Especially because he won, he did. You can't deny it. And now he has to fight again? He'll kill me and then fuck my corpse."

The Adjudicator gave a huff of amusement. "Ashe said you might have reservations. Very well. You'll be under my protection, safe from the heirs and every other fae. You will have your own apartments in the castle and the freedom to come and go as you please. We will consider you an honoured guest rather than a usurping enemy of the kingdom, and you will be free to leave once the Sword is crowned."

Ember's mind whirled. She had no choice. She could see that. An eternity of torture at the hands of a creature so foul, so hideous, that even the worst nightmares couldn't compare? No, thanks. But she had something he wanted, something everyone wanted. She could use that. She flicked her hair back, tied her robe, adopted a supercilious expression. "So, the bare minimum, then? What else do I get?"

The Adjudicator narrowed his eyes, the crepey folds becoming even more pronounced. "You surprise me."

"I want to return to Earth to a time of my choosing." Time in the fae world moved slower than the human world. Who knew how long the new tournament would take? Ember had no intention of returning to a world where all her new friends and clients were long dead.

"Agreed."

He made to raise a hand, but Ember interrupted, "I haven't finished. I also want a deposit of ten million dollars in my bank account. Earth money, not fae gold. And paperwork to prove its legality." Just her luck to be arrested for money laundering as soon as she got back. "And I want to take my glamour brush that Alena gave me." It had saved her life once, and she had no intention of leaving it behind. "And ..." she couldn't think. "I don't want to be included in the teams." Her presence on Cole's team had helped him win the tournament, and she was damned if she was going to be a part of that again.

He waited, but she had run out of things to ask for, and when she spoke no more, he snapped his fingers.

"Done."

# CHAPTER 3

Ember found travelling through the veil under the Adjudicator's power was a much easier journey than when she'd done it herself, with only Tana the Blade in the pendant to help her on her way. Then she'd been fighting through sludge. Now, it was as though she was flying on the seed of a dandelion, a wafting sensation of lightness in a white nothingness.

Soon, there came the sensation of stability under her feet, and she stumbled forward, the disconcerting displacement of time and space always a challenging balancing act. She looked around, nerves heightened, already coming into a defensive pose, one foot in front of the other, fists clenched. But her nerves settled as she took in her surroundings: an airy room with stone walls in mellow cream, palm trees flanking immense windows with white sheer drapes billowing gently in the sweet-scented breeze, diamond candelabras overhead, and white embroidered mats covering the wooden floor. There was an enormous fourposter bed taking up one end of the room, and a couple of areas for sitting and relaxing. An open door gave a glimpse of a bathroom, and standing by the outer door was a fae servant, clad unobtrusively in shades of coffee and cream—to match the room,

Ember supposed. His wings rose high in gorgeous tones of amber and blue and she remembered another pair of wings, the colours of a tropical bird, painted by the glamour brush that now rested on a low table by the bed.

She nodded at him and smiled. "Hello. I'm Ember."

He gave a shallow bow. His demeanour was almost disapproving, but his tone was polite as he said, "Welcome back, my lady."

"Thank you."

"Would you like some refreshment?"

It may have been daylight in the kingdom, but Ember's body-clock was closing in on midnight and she was shattered. "I'd just like to rest."

"Certainly," he said, and abruptly departed, closing the door with a sharp click behind him, as though he couldn't bear to be in the room with her a moment longer.

She was too tired to wonder at that. She crossed to the window, intending to pull the drapes closed, though they were so sheer they likely wouldn't block out an iota of light, but the view was arresting, and she leaned on the sill to look out over the castle grounds.

Her old rooms had looked out over a peaceful formal park with a distant view of the mountains that surrounded the neighbouring Kingdom of Stones. This room had an immediate view of the castle's utility areas: stables, a forge, kitchen gardens and the like. Beyond that, over the high castle walls, lay placid pastures, pockets of wild forest and a shimmering blue lake. Noises of hammering and voices and horses' hooves drifted up to her. The Adjudicator may have labelled her an honoured guest, but he'd put her in the noisiest wing of the castle.

The bed was soft and smelled like flowers. She slept.

"The Adjudicator is expecting you for dinner," came a smooth voice and she sat bolt upright, realising all at once that she wasn't in her bedroom. She was back in the land of the fae, and the corner of her mouth was sticky with drool. She wiped at her face and blinked drowsily. The light streaming through the windows was the soft light of morning; she'd slept for a long time. Her servant had a bundle of fabric in his arms, all pastels and gold ribbons, and she eyed it warily.

"Is that clothes?"

His raised eyebrow said, "no kidding, dummy," and her hackles rose a little, but she schooled her expression and threw back the tangle of sheets.

"I'd prefer to wear something else," she said firmly. "Something a little more practical, more ... black. Also, what should I call you?"

"I'm Gelen." He crossed to a closet standing in the corner of the room and swung open the door. He took out a black, military-style suit of leather and velvet on a hanger and held it up with an expression of distaste. "This?"

"Perfect."

Gelen slung the dresses into the closet without bothering to hang anything and shut the door. Ember could bet if she opened the door again, the closet would be empty, and the dresses whisked away to who-knew-where.

She took the suit and went into the bathroom. To her surprise, the bathroom was in the open air, and the only thing separating her from the rest of the world was a high wall covered with vines and flowers. Overhead, puffy white clouds tinged with the pink of dawn hung in a pale blue sky. Warm water sprayed from a wide faucet jutting from the wall, looking like a waterfall surrounded by hanging ferns and orchids.

The bathtub had already been filled, and rose petals floated atop the steaming water.

She ignored the bath, used the toilet, and then took a quick shower. All the luxuries of the castle that had delighted her in the past just seemed extravagant and annoying now. What a waste of bathwater, she thought, as she stepped out of the shower, giving her spiky hair a quick rub with a towel. She didn't even bother styling it anymore, just ran her fingers through it and left it to air-dry.

The uniform was sleek and close-fitting, and she paused for a moment in front of the mirror, checking that it didn't exaggerate her curves, didn't look as though she was cos-playing a slutty soldier or something. But she looked strong, uncompromising, militant. She didn't look like the girl who had first arrived in fae, all wide-eyed innocence in frills and high heels. She looked more like a wary cat.

She padded back into the room, sliding her glamour brush into her sleeve, and asking Gelen for a pair of boots which he produced within moments, with a little curl of his lip as though he thought little of her taste.

"Tell me about dinner," she said to Gelen. "The Adjudicator will be there, and who else?"

He shrugged. "I'm afraid I'm not privy to that information."

"Bullshit," she thought, but she didn't argue. Servants knew everything. Perhaps Gelen wanted her to be put off her guard, or perhaps he was hoping to intimidate her. The thing was, she didn't intimidate easily anymore.

"I'm sorry you're not at that level yet," she said instead, her voice as smooth as silk, her hand going up to caress the pendant around her neck. "I'll speak to the Adjudicator for you."

"No," he blurted, and she was pleased to see the colour drain from his face. "I remember them saying that it was going to be a dinner in the ballroom with the heirs and the teams."

"Thank you."

She sank onto a couch and extended her foot so that he had to get on his knees to wrap her soft foot coverings before lacing her boots. The power play was petty of her, but she didn't care. Gelen could make her life here very difficult if he had a mind to, and that was another hassle she didn't need. If they weren't to be friends, then he had better remember she had the pendant. She held the kingdom around her neck. For now, at least.

# CHAPTER 4

With a full day to kill until dinner that evening, Ember wasn't going to spend it in her room with Gelen glaring at her. She went into the hallway and called for a guide, a little glowing ball of light that would take her wherever she needed to go. The castle was vast. Some areas were exclusive to Cole, his supporters, and servants, some exclusive to Ashe, with the rest common to all. She wasn't familiar with this part of the castle, and with the Adjudicator's promise that no area was off-limits to her, she had no intention of accidentally straying into Cole's territory.

The guide soon came zipping along the hallway to meet her and she asked it to take her to the forest. "But," she added, "can you take me on a secret way?"

The guide bobbed up and down in what she assumed was assent, and she followed it a few paces down the hall, before it abruptly went sideways through the wood-panelled wall. Great.

She pressed her lips against the wall and called out, "Oi, I can't get through solid wood, you idiot."

Ember took a step back and waited, but the guide didn't reappear. She stared at the wall in consternation and tentatively touched it, pressing it all over, looking for some catch or mechanism. Her hunch paid off. As soon as her fingers tapped an indentation where one panel joined another, the two panels slid silently open. The guide waited just inside, its light filling the dark space, and she wagged her finger at it.

"Alright, smartie. You got me."

She climbed into the recess and the door slid shut behind her. The ceiling was only just higher than her head, and she could touch the stone walls on either side without extending her arms full length. She took a few deep breaths, not entirely comfortable in such a cramped space. The dark tunnel stretched in both directions, and she was glad the guide was with her. It bobbed ahead, and she followed it.

Occasionally, a hole in the wall showed a pinprick of light, and she could peek through. She saw a huge dining room, a space much more utilitarian that she was used to seeing in the castle, with rough benches and tables, and a couple of mops swishing water around the floor all by themselves. Then came more corridors with fae hurrying about on errands, and another room with each wall displaying colourful maps of the different kingdoms of Esha: Swords, Seeds, Stones, Skies and Sands. Heavy black smears obliterated one map, and she guessed that was the fallen kingdom, the one that the Swords had destroyed, the Kingdom of Shields.

She and the guide continued on, the tunnel twisting and turning and occasionally reaching a junction of two or three more tunnels heading off into the dark. Eventually though, the guide stopped, sliding sideways through the wall, and she spent a few heart-stopping moments in the pitch black as she fumbled for the opening mechanism, pressing with her fingers, and then thumping with the heel of her hand. Panic rose in her. She was going to be left here in the dark, forced to wander alone until she starved to death, her rotting corpse eventually adorning the tunnel with bones ... and then the wall slid open.

She emerged into soft green light, the forest spread before her. The guide bobbed up and down as if pleased she had arrived in one piece and shot off through the trees.

Her uniform was covered in dust, and she had a thin skein of cobwebs in her hair. She brushed at herself vigorously, wiping the webs on the nearest tree bark, trying not to think about the spiders who'd made them. Spiders in fae were *massive*.

Alena, the entity who lived in the forest, always presented herself immaculately. She was Ember's only friend in this place. Although, if she thought about it, she wasn't entirely sure if Alena really *was* a friend. An ally, perhaps. Either way, she didn't want to look too dishevelled in front of her. Alena was always elegant, and not especially known for her diplomacy.

Ember turned about to get her bearings and then struck down a winding path, enjoying the calming green of the trees and ferns. She passed the four columns that represented the still-standing kingdoms and the pile of rubble that represented the Shields, and eventually found herself at Alena's mirrored pool. A strange collection of hillocks and bumps buried under a thick carpet of moss lay on the opposite side, and she shivered as the glint of silver armour caught her eye. The forest had once acted to save her, smothering her enemies, and they evidently still lay here, untouched, unmourned.

She sank down beside the pool and dabbled her fingers in the water. The ripples she made grew bigger and water sloshed against the bank as a head broke the surface. Ember got to her feet as Alena stepped onto the grass, her silver hair coiled back into a smooth chignon, her dress reflecting both silver and green as she moved.

"My dear," Alena said without preamble, "I thought you'd left."

"Hello," said Ember. She felt a little shy. Alena had the presence of a queen, the caustic tongue of a fishwife, and power rivalling Cole and Ashe. Ember preferred to remain in her good graces. Quickly, she summarised the situation. "They found me. They want the pendant, but none of them will take it. The princes have to battle for it."

Alena narrowed her eyes. "Which means the Blade inside has bonded himself to you. Fascinating."

"What does that mean?"

Alena shrugged. "Without a true Sword, he's latched onto the closest thing. That's you. You won't have the power of the Sword, but you'll certainly be able to call on the Blade if you need him. Which is good, considering Cole has run quite mad."

Ember couldn't help the shiver that ran down her back. "I'm not responsible for his actions."

"I believe you, my dear. It's just the rest of fae that doesn't."

"The Adjudicator has promised my safety while I'm here."

Alena made a scoffing noise. "Promises are like summer—the winter comes eventually. You're a fool to come back, but I suppose you had no choice in the matter."

"Not really."

"It wouldn't have been so bad if you hadn't had sex with him." Alena laughed as Ember's face grew hot. "Tell me truly, do you know what it's like for a fae to lie with a human?"

"I know what it was like for me," she said shortly. Pleasure past the point of pain, where venom laced every soft touch, every sweet kiss. Cole had twisted her, warped her. His need for her had stolen her memories and her will, until she had been nothing but an empty vessel for him to exhaust his passion, and she had revelled in every moment, a willing slave. She closed her mind to the memories. She wasn't that person anymore.

"You are an addiction. You are everything he can never be. Your human innocence is like a drug to him. He must consume and consume. No fae woman will satisfy him as you did. He loved you and he's lost you. But he'll never stop wanting you."

"He never loved me," Ember corrected her. "He used me. Obsession and possession are not love."

Alena's eyes twinkled. "And tell me, little one, what is love for you?"

"Love is giving. And kindness. And selflessness."

"You loved him, then."

Ember shrugged. "I did, and then I didn't."

"And nevermore will you." It was as though Alena was chanting a spell, a vow, a declaration to the world, and the ringing words made Ember's blood race and her heart pound. The water in the pool rose into a shimmering tower, whirled about and crashed down again, splashing them with foam. "Do you want to see what he's done?"

Ember shook her head emphatically.

"You should. Because then you'll understand your situation a little better. I don't quite think you know what you've got yourself into." She pointed through the trees to a stone archway, one unfamiliar to Ember. "I hope you've got the stomach for it."

She gently stroked a finger down Ember's cheek. Her touch felt slightly clammy. And then she stepped back into the pool and sank below the surface.

Ember took a deep breath. Discovering what Cole had done was the last thing she wanted to do, but she trusted Alena, and she needed to know everything. Tentatively, with grudging steps, she approached the archway, reluctant to leave the gentle forest behind.

# CHAPTER 5

As Ember passed under the archway, the warmth of the forest gave way to the chill of stone corridors. The sound of her boots padding down the hall reverberated off the walls and ceiling, a steady *thump, thump* that did nothing for her peace of mind. She retreated to the wall, one hand grazing the stone, gaze darting back and forth, starting as faint shadows danced in the light thrown by the candelabras overhead, which vanished as she drew closer. Occasionally she passed a door set into the wall, embossed with the kingdom's sigil of two crossed swords. By reflex, she clutched the orange jewel around her neck tight, as if it were a talisman of protection.

The corridor turned a sharp corner and abruptly opened onto a long mezzanine floor. She leaned on the polished railing, looking down on a room with plush chairs dotted about little tables and colourful silk banners hanging on the walls. It was a sitting room designed for discussion and leisure, but right now there was no conversation, for the room was empty.

She turned away, and her eyes widened. Paintings hung on the walls of the mezzanine, familiar paintings, for they looked to be those that she herself had painted, practice pieces which were very different from the gothic style pictures she had presented at the last student exhibition. She stepped closer to examine them. The nearest one was a study of her little kitchen and the clutter on her kitchen table. She had painted it soon after arriving in her new city, and it represented freedom and domesticity with the golden light of the evening streaming through the window. She didn't enjoy looking back at her work, for she always found something she could have done better, but this was one of the few pieces that she'd never wanted to change.

Except ...

This wasn't her picture. The details were off. Way off. The apples in the bowl showed hideous, snarling faces in the reflective shine of their skins. The snapdragons in the vase grimaced with bloodied fangs, their graceful stems bristling with thorns. The careless newspaper on the table didn't feature the picture of the athlete crossing the finish line that she had originally painted. It was a fae instead, sprawled lifeless on the ground in a crumpled tangle of limbs, and it had little Lily's face, Ember's friend, whom Cole had killed.

She gave a little cry, her gaze flicking to another painting and then another. All had been subtly warped and twisted. A tree with a screaming face in the bark, people with torn flesh exposing ragged tendons and gleaming bones, a cat—a zombie cat—with maggots spilling from its eyes.

Closing her eyes, she turned away from the paintings. There was only one she knew who would reduce her paintings to hideous mimicry, who had enough power to peer through the void between their worlds and watch what she was doing. The thought that Cole had been spying all this time was terrifying.

Was this what Alena had wanted her to see? A collection of fake art? A door lay at the end of the mezzanine, and she edged toward it, not really wanting to go on, but feeling compelled to, as if someone were pulling her by a thin, silken ribbon. When she came to the door at the end, she gently pushed it open and entered, only to be brought up short in horror.

It was the smell that hit her first, the rusty, metallic smell of old blood and shit and piss from the bodies that littered the ground. She gagged and retched, unable to comprehend the sheer magnitude of death and suffering that lay before her. Pale lips peeled back in silent screams, teeth bared, wings shredded, limbs severed, heads separated from torsos, innards spilled on the polished floorboards. It was a slaughterhouse. Broken fae lay everywhere, some slumped against the wall, others piled in heaps as though making a path for someone coming through. And smeared on the wall in their lifeblood, a single word.

*Traitor.*

Ember stood there for an endless moment before backing out, and then she broke into a run as if to escape the images of those hacked-up bodies, but it was impossible. They were already burned into her mind.

She fled the mezzanine, turned a corner and then another, and eventually came to a stop, leaning against the stone wall, chest heaving. She bent and spat on the floor, the taste of death staining her mouth.

It took some time before she gathered wits enough to look around to see where she was. She decided to call a guide, and then to her surprise, realised she knew this place. She'd been here before. She pushed off the wall, wiping at the cold tears on her cheeks, and continued down the hall to a door with an iron moulding of a tree set into the wood panel. Slowly, she turned the handle and entered.

The last time she'd been here, hundreds of fae crowded the room around a gigantic tree with leaves that burned and blazed, the tree that signified the end of the old reign and the beginning of the new. But now the fire was extinguished, the leaves crumbled, the twisted limbs of the tree blackened and broken.

She felt something move at her chest and she swiped at her uniform, startled, thinking that perhaps some creepy crawly was climbing up to her neck. But it was the pendant around her neck, throbbing and twitching, as though Tana, the Blade inside, knew where he was.

The tree was a symbol for her too, she thought, a symbol of death. A sign that nothing remained for here. All at once she understood what Alena hadn't told her, that the fae felt she was responsible for the madness of the heir and the murder of his subjects. Not Cole, their handsome, charming, erratic prince, but her. No wonder Gelen had looked at her as though he hated her.

In her head, she knew that was bullshit. She'd been through enough therapy to know that an abuser's actions were one hundred percent on them. She wasn't responsible. And if she hadn't stolen the pendant, if she hadn't done what she'd felt she had to, she wouldn't have been able to go home.

Although she was here now, so it had been for nothing anyway.

She turned away, intending to go back to her room and wash away the horrors she'd seen, the taint of death that clung to her clothes and flesh. But a familiar figure was lounging in the doorway watching her, and she gave a startled cry.

Cole.

# Chapter 6

Her automatic response was to run, to get the fuck out of there *now*, but she knew nothing would give him more satisfaction. So, she drew herself up and folded her arms, adopting the sulky, rebellious stance of a teenager caught ditching school. She had the Adjudicator behind her. He had promised the heirs wouldn't harm her. And yet, her mind whispered unhelpfully, had he told Cole about that?

Cole wore his habitual light colours of desert sands, the golden fairytale prince with a white sword at his side. High cheekbones, perfectly carved lips, green eyes blazing. He looked as beautiful as he ever did, but there were shadows beneath his eyes, and his hands were convulsively clenching and unclenching, as though he was preparing to fight with his fists and then reminding himself he shouldn't.

His gaze roamed over her hungrily, taking in the slim fitted uniform, the new spiky hair, and finally, the pendant hanging around her neck. When he spoke, his tone was bitter. "I didn't think you'd come back."

"I had no choice." Her voice didn't have the commanding strength she'd intended. It cracked in the middle and there was a quaver that she couldn't control.

His nostrils flared, and his perfect lips curved in a smile. He knew she was terrified. He could sense the fear in her, as though he were a hunting dog poised for attack.

She took a step back. Mistake. In a flash, he was in front of her, fingers biting cruelly into her upper arms, preventing any escape. She tried to break free, but he dragged her to him. She inhaled his scent and was immediately transported back through a kaleidoscope of muddled memories: tangled sheets, pleasure whips, heated flesh, and the sweet torture of unfulfilled desire made complete. He gently nuzzled her, his lips at her neck, trailing fire up to her earlobe. One hand slid around her back and down to her buttocks and he pulled her closer to him so she could feel his rising desire. She felt lips at her ear, his breath warm as he whispered, "I've never hated anyone so much."

He kissed her then, a kiss that bruised and hurt, and she couldn't help responding even as she twisted to get away. Her thoughts were whirling, her limbs becoming liquid. She hated him too, hated what he'd done to her. He'd turned her into a helpless plaything, dependent on his whim, and it had taken everything she had to escape him. She loathed him, but it didn't appear her body had got the message. Lust, like a venomous snake, coiled in the pit of her stomach. She hadn't taken a lover since him, and all at once she yearned to be touched, explored, taken.

"You missed me," he murmured, and it wasn't a question, but a statement of fact.

She didn't answer but kissed him back, as aggressive as he, biting his lower lip, feeling him smile. She slid her hands into his hair and yanked hard, wanting to hurt him, pleased when the breath hissed out of him, and he groaned against her mouth. He wasn't used to her fighting back, and clearly, he liked it. But there was something else too, an uncomfortable warmth at her breastbone, a warmth that was becoming hotter and hotter, a laser burning through her jacket into her flesh.

There was a thunderous *crack*, and Cole flew back through the air, flung by an invisible hand. He landed awkwardly, staggering slightly, and looked down at himself. A burned hole in his clothing, ringed with black, revealed skin once a golden tan, now unpleasantly red. Smoke coiled lazily up from the singed fabric.

The pendant was cool, no longer the living coal it had been, and her clothing was unmarked. She touched the jewel warily, but the fire had been extinguished. Fighting the urge to touch her lips to see how bruised and swollen they were, she eyed Cole. She could taste blood in her mouth, and it nauseated her.

His lip twisted, his eyes following the movement of her fingers, and his hand went to the white sword at his side. "You wear that without honour. You really are a disgusting creature."

His breathing was quick, and she could see the effect she'd had on him, outlined clearly against his pants. He may think her disgusting, but Alena had been right. He still wanted her.

She gave a careless shrug, but his words stung. She'd taken it to save her life. More than that, she'd taken it to save the kingdom from Cole, as well as her own home. She hadn't forgotten Lissa's cryptic words, "Esha isn't the only world served by the Sword." She'd had three years to ponder them before concluding that perhaps Cole had designs on not just ruling his own kingdom but Earth as well. An image of crumpled, torn bodies floated into her mind, and she shook her head, as if to force the memory out. For all her best intentions, many innocents had suffered under Cole's hand.

"Still, perhaps the winning will be much sweeter once you're forced to hand it over," he continued. "And why are you dressed like that? Have you become a clone of Ashe in practice and in thought?"

She blinked at him, the barbs about her clothes slipping past her entirely as she latched onto his first words. "Why would I hand it over to you? Ashe might win."

"I won already. Two games from three. The pendant is mine."

"Yes," she said automatically, but her mind was racing. The Adjudicator hadn't told him he had to battle again. He'd omitted that little nugget. Why? Ashe knew. Or rather, Ashe had guessed. Cole apparently thought his rulership was a foregone conclusion and, after what she'd seen, she certainly wasn't going to be the one to tell him he was wrong.

"Stupid woman," Cole said conversationally. "Did you forget?"

His contempt was blatant, but he couldn't take his eyes from her, the naked desire plain on his face. She ran a hand through her hair and watched him shiver and she wondered if he was imagining his own hands in her hair as she knelt in front of him, took him in her mouth and —

The pendant began to warm; she could feel it the heat of it, a warning.

"I must go." There was a door at the far end, past the burned, broken tree, and she edged toward it, not wanting to walk past him the way she'd come. She could call a guide when she was safe.

"Oh yes," he said, and his tone was casual, as though they were merely acquaintances meeting on the street. "Go and paint something pretty. I'll see you at dinner. And remember, Ember, a part of me still runs through your veins."

He watched her go, and she forced herself to walk slowly, casually. She wasn't entirely sure he wouldn't follow, and when she finally reached the door, scrabbling for the handle and slipping through, she slammed it behind her and then ran, as if all the demons in hell were chasing her.

# CHAPTER 7

S he sprinted back to her room, so unnerved that she almost over-
took the guide, and when she finally got there, she went straight
to the bathroom, ignoring Gelen's bow as she passed. She tugged off
her clothes and stood under an icy spray of water, seething. When
she felt as though she'd punished herself enough, she warmed the
water and tried to relax, doing the breathing exercises her therapist
had taught her. Three years, she thought bitterly, as she counted off
slowly, inhaling, exhaling. Three years of hard work and he'd undone
it all with one kiss. She lowered the temperature of the water again and
glowered.

Eventually though, she had to come out. She wrapped a fluffy white
towel around her and brushed her teeth until her gums were sore.
When she padded back into the room, Gelen bowed deep again, a
hint of alarm in his eyes. Clearly, he thought she was unhinged. She
brusquely asked him for a clean uniform and something to eat, and he
leaped to retrieve both.

She was pleasantly surprised to find that this fresh change of clothes
now had a slender pocket concealed on her sleeve, exactly the size
to carry her glamour brush. When she thanked Gelen, he merely

shrugged as if it wasn't his doing at all and, considering she had a magical closet in the corner, it probably wasn't.

Once dressed, she stood at the window and watched the bustle in the courtyard below. Young maids gossiped in a shadowy corner, giggling as they watched three young male fae unloading a wagon, their foreheads glowing with perspiration and muscles straining under the weight of sacks and barrels. Two centaurs trotted over the cobblestones, their hooves thrumming a cheerful tattoo against the flagstones. A woman threw grain for a flock of fat birds in a pen, while another picked a basket of herbs from a walled off garden, little glowing lights hovering above the flowers showing where tiny fairies liked to swarm.

The sight of domesticity was calming, and as she watched, she nibbled at the corner of a piece of bread smothered in some kind of meat paste and then drank some tea. Afterwards she felt better, but she couldn't help restlessly going over and over her meeting with Cole.

Cole didn't know he had to face Ashe in battle. The Adjudicator was probably saving that little tidbit for dinner, which meant that Ember had better make sure she wasn't seated anywhere near him. She wouldn't put it past him to strangle her in front of everyone.

'A part of me still runs through your veins,' he'd said, and that was another thing he didn't know. His magic hadn't worked on her. All his other teammates had taken in his power, had used it to fight in the tournament. But somehow, she'd fought against it. He was no more a part of her than she was a part of the floor, or a horse, or whatever. He held no power over her. And yet …

The memory of the kiss came unbidden, and she flushed. What had she been thinking? She'd literally just seen dead bodies, piles and piles of them, all victims of Cole's wrath, and the memory of them had flown out of her head as soon as Cole touched her. He was right. She was a disgusting creature. She disgusted herself. And along with her own self-disgust came a burning hatred for Cole. If she ever got the power and the opportunity, she would quite happily kill him.

Abruptly, she asked Gelen to fetch some wine. Alcohol seemed like a great idea.

"My lady," Gelen murmured as he held out a crystal glass on a gold tray. She took it, and knocked back half of it in one gulp, closing her eyes as the familiar fizz of bubbles on her tongue became a steady glow of warmth in her stomach.

"Thank you. Sorry for being so rude. It's just weird being back."

He looked taken aback at that and shook his head. "You should behave as you see fit."

"I saw what he did. What the heir did."

He must have known what exactly she meant, for his posture stiffened and his demeanour became even more frigid. "Yes, my lady."

"It was a terrible thing. I'm so very sorry."

He nodded but didn't reply, his face expressionless.

She wished he'd drop the impersonal demeanour. She needed a friend. "I had a maid when I was here last. Her name was —"

"Lily." His voice was soft. "She is missed."

"I thought I might try to find her family. And tell them ... tell them how good she was, how sweet."

She'd always wanted to talk to Lily's parents. Not just to tell them how much she loved Lily, but also ... *to soothe your conscience*, the nasty part of her mind muttered. She blocked it out. "Do you know the village she came from? She said it was nearby."

He looked at her, confusion in his eyes. "Of course, my lady. Grey-clare. Although I'm not sure if it would be safe for you to travel there. The kingdom is in some disarray."

"What do you mean, disarray?"

"There is no Sword," he said simply. "We're all dependent on a kingly arse sitting on the throne."

She raised her eyebrows at his irreverent tone, and he gulped, his face pale. "I do apologise."

"It's fine," she said, giving him a quick grin. "I don't actually care about all the 'my lady's' and the bowing and all the rest of it. And I'm not going to run off and tell the Adjudicator either."

"What I meant to say was, without a Sword, without a leader, our kingdom becomes vulnerable to the others. They circle, they take little testing bites, and then if they get no response, they might gobble us up." He eyed her speculatively, his gaze drifting down to the pendant. "Are you to be our Sword, my lady?"

"No. No way. I'm just a—" *thief* "—caretaker, I guess."

He nodded, and waited, a little awkwardly, until she said he could go. Breaking the ice with Gelen was proving to be tougher than she'd thought.

She remained in her room for the rest of the day, amusing herself by calling for canvas and paints and trying to paint Lily from memory. Losing herself in her work was therapeutic and calming, and when the light finally faded and it was near time for dinner, she washed the paint from her hands, slid them wet through her hair to make it stick up a little more and took a deep breath.

Showtime.

# Chapter 8

Gelen had changed into a soft black tunic and trousers to complement Ember's outfit. In the darkness of the candlelit halls, his pale hands and face looked as though floating in space. She wasn't sure whether he was thawing toward her or if his job required him to look like her, but she appreciated it.

He had assumed he was escorting her to the ballroom alone, but she called for a posse of guards as well. After what had happened with Cole earlier, she wasn't taking any chances that he might be lying in wait for her. But the halls were relatively clear, and any random fae hurrying about their business took one look at her entourage and darted the other way.

Guards in silver armour were stationed at the ballroom's immense double doors, and they flung them open as she approached. Her palms were wet with nervous sweat, and her heart was pounding uncomfortably hard, but she schooled her face into a bland expression and forced herself to wait as she took in the room.

Live statues draped in gauzy gold lined the walls: dancers with muscles flexed in attitudes of impossible dexterity, unmoving. A long table stood to one side, a blazing vision in gold, the formal setting customary with any important dinner in the castle. Guests sat and chattered, all clad in bright colours and flimsy fabrics, jewels winking in the light. Their voices died as they saw Ember standing framed in the doorway, and all was silent as she finally strolled forward.

The Adjudicator stood at one end of the table, his cohort of jurors arrayed behind him, all faceless behind dark red cowls, an aura of foreboding rising from them.

"My dear." He beckoned to her with a withered hand. "You must sit beside me."

This was the last thing she wanted to do, but as she saw the naked animosity emanating from every single being at the table, she fairly scuttled toward him, easing herself onto the empty gold chair next to him as Gelen took up position against the wall behind her. She looked down at her lap, pretending to smooth the fabric of her pants, which of course, was completely unnecessary, and sucking in a shaky breath, looked up.

She recognised many at the table. All had been in the heirs' teams, all survivors of the deadly tournament. The absence of Broude, the handsome winged fae who'd fallen in his match, cut her like a knife. But there was Swirl, the centaur who had been so kind to her, and she gave him a tentative smile. His eyes were warm as he nodded gravely back, which made her feel a little better. And then her gaze fell on Cole, who was staring at her with such a raw blend of hatred and lust that she felt it like a fiery arrow to her abdomen.

Ashe sat opposite him, stern and upright, his habitual black uniform as out of place in the colourful crowd as her own. He didn't so much as glance at her, and she wasn't sure what to make of that.

Perhaps he too hated her as much as Cole but had decorum enough to hide it.

Cole raised his glass and called down the table to her. "And here she is. Once again, I apologise profusely to all here for bringing this viper into our midst. If I'd known what a treacherous creature she was, I would never have considered it. Adjudicator, I thank you for restoring her to fae justice."

Ember couldn't help herself. She gave him a mocking smile and blew him a kiss.

The superior look on Cole's face vanished. His eyes narrowed and his lip curled, hands gripping the edge of the table so hard his knuckles were white. He looked as though he might launch himself down the table at her.

She raised an eyebrow, mocking. *Do it.*

"Don't let her tempt you into dishonour, cousin," came Ashe's slow drawl. "This isn't the time or place."

Cole glared at him. "I draw the line at having to eat with her."

"And yet," Ember couldn't resist saying, "you were happy enough to stick your tongue down my throat earlier."

There was a gasp around the table. Ashe's gaze flicked to her, dark and cold. Cole pushed his chair back with the shriek of metal against wood and surged to his feet. Ashe was on his feet too, a ball of fire already whirling in his hand. Everyone else looked as though they were preparing to dive for cover. Ember's heart hammered in her chest, in tandem with the pendant twitching nervously against her breastbone. She had pushed him too far; she was going to die for her insolence ...

The Adjudicator raised a hand. "No fighting before dinner."

There was a breathless pause and then Cole sat with a graceless thump, followed by Ashe, the fire in his hand quenched. Tentatively, the conversation started up again as though nothing had happened, although the tension remained.

A servant came forward to pour Ember a goblet of wine. She lifted the heavy cup, willing her hand to not betray her by trembling, and drank deep. She was going to need it.

The water sprite on the other side of her gave her a shy smile. "Hello."

A memory flashed into Ember's mind, of another impossibly beautiful water sprite who'd tried to kill her, and she flinched, thinking that Lissa had somehow come back to life. But no. This wasn't Lissa. She looked familiar though and after a moment or two, Ember placed her as the sprite who had helped her in her game. She smiled with the relief of recognition and nodded back. "Hello."

"Fayla," the sprite said. "I don't think we ever got around to names." She wore a light blue gown shot with gold. It complemented her skin, which was of an even lighter blue, traced over with soft yellow scales.

"I'm Ember," Ember said.

"I know." Fayla's gaze drifted to the pendant around Ember's neck and then shot up to her face again. She lowered her voice. "Is there to be a new tournament? Is that why we're all here?"

To Ember's surprise, she looked excited by the prospect, as if fighting for someone else's honour—to the *death*—was the most thrilling thing ever. Ember couldn't understand that. Fayla had only just survived the tournament and yet she looked eager to tempt death again.

Ember shrugged. "I'm not sure."

Music sounded around the hall, mellow and melodic. Servants marched into the room carrying covered gold platters of food, one for each diner. When Ember's plate was placed in front of her and the cover whisked off, she was surprised and gratified to find golden roast chicken pieces with all the trimmings: gravy, mashed potato, and fresh greens. Fayla was tucking into a whole, poached fish, while further down the table, Swirl the centaur had what looked like a hot mash.

Ember was about to cut into the chicken with her knife, when the meat flickered as if it were a video that had glitched. She froze. The chicken had transformed into some kind of green reptile with charred, scaly skin. She gave it a tentative poke with her fork, and it was back to golden skinned chicken, tender and delicious.

"All well?" came a raspy voice. The Adjudicator was watching her carefully. His plate was empty of food, as if he didn't feel the need to do anything as commonplace as eating, and she nodded, not wanting him to know she knew her dinner was glamoured, that her chicken was really something else. Besides, if she didn't stare directly at it, it still looked like chicken.

"Oh no, I'm fine. Thank you." She carved off a small bite, putting it into her mouth. Tasted like chicken anyhow.

He smiled, and she suppressed a shudder. He wasn't at his best when he smiled.

The diners chattered in low voices as they ate, each stealing glances down the table toward her. She kept her gaze firmly on her plate and ate her reptile, bite by bite, although she wasn't really hungry anymore. She was just doing it automatically to keep her strength up in case she had to make a break for it, while magical fireballs whizzed around the room. She considered her knife, wondering if she should slip it into the brush pocket on her sleeve, just in case.

The desserts arrived, parfait concoctions of pink and white, webbed with a lacework of spun sugar, the middles filled with cream. Then came cheese and crisp breads for anyone who still had room, and small glasses filled with sweet liqueurs.

The conversation limped along and eventually came to a faltering stop. As if on cue, the Adjudicator rose to his feet, and the red cloaked jurors stepped forward to flank him on either side.

"Well, isn't this nice?" he said, ignoring the incredulous side-eyes flickering around the table. "All together again. The tree shall be re-lit with a special ceremony to mark the new contest. The ceremony will—"

Here we go, thought Ember, as Cole surged to his feet, and she closed a hand over her fork, concealing it down by her side.

"What do you mean, a new contest?" Cole bellowed at the Adjudicator, anger overriding all propriety. "There is no need for another tournament. I won. I won!" He glared around the table. "You all know I did. So, make her give me the pendant, make Ashe the Blade and have done with this tawdry charade."

The Adjudicator gave a wintry smile. "The Blade unfortunately bonded with her when she stole it away. Therefore, it must be won again."

"She isn't an heir! How could it bond with her?" Cole shouted.

"You weren't an heir either, once upon a time," the Adjudicator said smoothly. "Isn't that right, Ashe?"

Ember glanced at Ashe curiously. His lips were pressed tightly together, his jaw set, the colour drained from his face. If she wasn't mistaken, the Adjudicator was talking about Cole's sister, Serafina. She had died and Cole had stepped into her place. Ember hadn't known it had affected Ashe so strongly.

"That's got nothing to do—" Cole began.

"The Treaty of the Swords was forged from deeper magic than you will ever know," said the Adjudicator, cutting him off. "The Blade bonded with her and has been given new life. He cannot die until a new Blade replaces him. The pendant must be won again."

The hall was silent, the guests, servants and motionless dancers all breathless with anticipation.

"This time, there will be no teams. Cole and Ashe will fight alone."

# CHAPTER 9

Horrified murmurs grew to aggrieved protests. Fayla burst into tears; her sobs smothered against her cupped hands.

The Adjudicator watched the commotion with a hint of smug satisfaction on his face and then raised a hand for silence. But if anything, the hubbub grew louder.

A centaur on Ashe's team, seemingly unable to help himself, backed away from the table and reared on his hind legs before crashing down again. His voice boomed through the hall. "This is against tradition! The teams stand with the heirs! It has always been so!"

A handsome male fae got to his feet, his wings flicking restlessly, raising him a metre or so off the ground. "The heir's power still runs through our veins. You cannot deny our chance to use it!"

Ember shivered. Imagine if Cole's power had taken hold of her at the games and still slithered around within her. It was bad enough that he could still command her body to lust. Still, that wasn't a true power. It was only that which she gave him, and she had to control it before he used it against her.

"The Treaty of Swords states …" the Adjudicator began, but a sprite interrupted him, jerking her head toward Ember,

"The treaty has already been overturned, thanks to her, and now you're shaming us by not allowing us our rightful place?"

The Adjudicator's mouth closed with a snap. It seemed to Ember that he was growing larger, darker, his craggy face suffused with fury. It was obvious he wasn't used to being interrupted. The jurors fanned out, advancing down the length of the table, their long robes concealing their footsteps, so they appeared to be gliding on wheels. As one, they turned to face the fae seated in front of each of them and raised red gloved hands. The sickening crack of necks snapping reverberated throughout the ballroom, followed by thuds as bodies slumped sideways to the floor or collapsed onto the table.

The silence was absolute.

"In the absence of a Sword, I am the power in this kingdom, and the human is the protector." The Adjudicator's gaze skated over Ember, and she felt it as an icy finger running down her back. "Heirs and supporters are sacrosanct until the contest. That is all."

He gave everyone one last withering glance and then moved out of the hall, his jurors fanning into place behind him.

Ember glanced at Fayla, who was still crying into the palms of her hands. Makeup streaked her face and fingers, and Ember wondered if she should say something of comfort, although what, she had no idea. Gelen, however, was already urging her from her seat, the formal mask of his profession barely concealing a look of terror in his eyes, and she hurriedly rose to leave.

"Once again, chaos reigns and it's all your fault," Cole hissed behind her, his voice as cutting as a whip, and she flinched but continued toward the doors, which suddenly felt like a very long way away.

"How now, cousin," Ashe drawled. "If you hadn't treated her like a whipped dog, you may have been the Sword now. Or not. Remember, she helped you on your way to victory—as empty as it was."

There was a crash of plates and cutlery as Cole threw himself across the table at Ashe, and then a mass fight erupted, with Cole's teammates trying to pull him off Ashe, and Ashe's teammates shouting encouragement. The Adjudicator may have ruled that lives were sacrosanct, but apparently, that didn't include a good brawl.

Others were making a hasty exit too, including the servants and dancers, and Ember found herself in a group of bodies fleeing for the door. They knocked her first to one side and then the other, and she wasn't entirely convinced that the shoving was accidental.

Swirl the centaur pushed through the crowd toward her and she leaned into him gratefully. "Get to your room. It'll not be safe for you."

"I'm under the protection of the Adjudicator." A spark of fire straightened her backbone, her chin lifting belligerently. "I have the pendant and apparently the Blade has bonded to me. And I'm sick of everyone treating me like I'm the plague or a princess."

"Pretty words," he said, with a hint of amusement. "But not as pretty when you've a knife shoved between your ribs. Get to your room."

The trip through the halls to her room was a quick one. Her stomach ached, but she wasn't sure if it was a stitch from running, an emotional reaction to the disastrous dinner, or the glamoured chicken. She asked Gelen for a soothing tea, and he readily complied, but he served it to her with a disapproving expression which grated on her nerves. Likely he blamed her for the deaths at dinner, even though they were nothing to do with her. She told him rather frostily that he'd better retire for the night, and she'd see him in the morning.

Without a word he left, and she drank her tea at the window, looking out into the starry night at the unfamiliar constellations above. How much longer was she to wait for the contest? And how on earth was she going to get through it?

# CHAPTER 10

S he dreamed she was teetering on the edge of a cavernous hole. A fire burned below, red and orange flames leaping high towards her. And then something cannoned into her, thrusting her forward into space, and she was falling, falling, the unbearable heat of the flames blistering her skin, her flesh peeling from her bones, and—

She woke in a sweat, a dazzling shaft of sunlight sneaking through a crack in the curtains to lie across her face. She felt weak and tired, and wondered if she was coming down with something. Her stomach still hadn't settled from the night before, and she refused Gelen's offer of breakfast, opting instead for a glass of cold juice and something to ease her nausea. He brought a vial of something resembling liquid silver, and she swallowed it before chasing it with the tart juice. After a few minutes, she felt well enough to get up.

After washing and dressing, she paced around the room for a bit, before deciding to pass the time by painting in the forest instead. With Swirl's warning still ringing in her ears, she asked Gelen for an escort of guards and as they swept through the halls, fae, servants and courtiers averted their eyes and moved swiftly out of the way as she passed.

Once she reached the forest, she asked for an easel and paints, took up position beside a gnarled tree, and set herself to recreate the whorls and folds of the bark. Her skills had improved markedly during her three-year stint at art school, and once again she lost herself in the act of creation, as familiar and yet new as ever. She filled the canvas with patterns of bark and, when it was done, set it aside to dry before picking up another canvas and attempting another with an intriguing pattern like a jigsaw.

Painting bark was an exercise she'd done many times back home. If faces appeared in the grain, she would deliberately accentuate them in black, so there was no mistake that they were supposed to be there. But this time she let the faces sit beneath the surface, refusing to let them rise to the top. The warped faces reminded her of the paintings in the gallery, the pictures that were hers and yet not hers, and all at once, she felt a perverse desire to see them again.

She let the brush drop, the second canvas only half complete, and motioned that the waiting guards and Gelen should follow. They passed under the archway, the tramp of the guards' boots echoing off the cold stone walls. Although she wondered at the wisdom of walking into a part of the castle that Cole frequented, she just couldn't help herself, and besides, there were witnesses now. The corridor turned the corner into the mezzanine gallery and all thoughts of Cole flew out of her head.

She studied the paintings for a time, lips pursed, head tilted to one side. They looked like AI art. No substance, no heart, no true feeling; just colours and shapes that almost fitted together. A small painting high on the wall attracted her attention. In her world, it was a self-portrait, with her face in half-shadow. Her tutor had said she looked as though she were lonely and yet perfectly happy about it. But here, the loneliness was transformed into an expression of depraved lust, eyes half closed in passion, a pink serpent's tongue creeping from the corner of her mouth to lick at a glistening smear across her lips, and she had no doubt what *that* was supposed to be.

She turned away, casually glancing into the room below, and almost had a heart attack. A group in red stood arrayed below, gazing up at her in silence. The Adjudicator, flanked by his jurors, waved a hand and she flinched as he appeared in front of her. The jurors hadn't moved, their red cowls tilted up toward her, and yet she still couldn't see their faces. Her guards and Gelen immediately moved to the wall, pressing their faces against it as if to render themselves invisible, and she wished she could do the same.

"I understand you were the inspiration for all of this," the Adjudicator said brightly, waving an expansive hand.

She didn't give him a reply, but it didn't appear as though he wanted one.

"It seems you've taken the attention of both the heirs ... and most of Esha." He reached out with a withered finger as if to touch the pendant hanging around her neck. She felt the stone quiver, and he dropped his hand. "Do you know anything about Esha? About where you are?"

"Not really. I sort of know where the kingdoms lie from what I can see from the castle windows, but ..."

"Oh, that won't do, my dear. You need a map."

She felt the ground tear itself from under her feet as if she were about to be dashed to the floor and she flung her arms out to steady herself. But the world became still, and she was somewhere different. Gelen and the guards were nowhere to be seen.

She stood in a room with a high domed ceiling, painted with what looked like islands in a shimmering blue sea. There were tables covered with parchment and inks, and walls lined with shelves of books. There were several fae there too, scrambling to press their faces against the shelves to be as unobtrusive as possible. Most of them wore dark green robes slit in the back to accommodate wings or tails, dusty with chalk, hands spotted with ink. Scholars, she supposed, although there were a few servants there too.

The Adjudicator led her over to a round table in the centre of the room, with a large map painted across it. He tapped on a grey castle outlined with gold on the upper right of the map. "Here is the Kingdom of Swords." The castle lay amongst rolling green hills and pockets of thick forest, a placid land dotted about with little villages.

He made a gesture, and the map swivelled and expanded, reminding Ember of the pinching outward movement she did on her phone to make a photo or article bigger. He pointed out a craggy range of mountains, and leaning over them, Ember could have sworn that she felt an icy mountain breeze touch her cheek, fresh and clean. "This is the Kingdom of Stones."

The map moved again as he showed her where the other kingdoms lay: the Seeds in dark green jungle beside a busy archipelago of green forested islands, Sands in the southern desert, and Skies—not nestled amongst the mountains as she might have thought—but near a bight, amongst a group of tall gleaming towers. There was an open green part of the map with gold lettering that said 'Free Grasslands' and she asked what it meant.

The Adjudicator gave a sniff. "Centaurs. That's their homeland."

Ember's eyebrows lifted in surprise. She'd always thought centaurs were citizens of the Kingdom of Swords. "I didn't know they had their own kingdom."

"If you can call grass and dirt a kingdom," the Adjudicator replied, and Ember had the feeling that no, he didn't.

The grasslands were vast, bordered by hills and forests, with the Seeds, Skies and Sands hovering nearby, and Ember wondered why Swirl lived with the Swords, so far away. Or perhaps he'd been born here? Had he ever been home? She'd have to ask.

A piece of the map looked as though it had been scorched, and she knew without asking that it marked the lost Kingdom of Shields, destroyed by the power of the Swords in a battle long ago. It was that battle that had forced the Swords to treaty. Unlike the other kingdoms ruled by a duo, the treaty only permitted one ruler of the Swords while the other was confined, for together, their power had been deemed too great. Tana was the previous Blade, trapped in the pendant that Ember wore around her neck. He would only be replaced once Cole or Ashe was crowned.

She glanced at the burned part of the map, squinted, and then frowned. There was a tiny spot of reddish brown in the centre of the burn. She looked closer, wondering if someone had spilled something on the map, a droplet of tea perhaps, but the spot looked painted on. When she looked closer, she could have sworn the spot was pulsating slightly, with a little rhythm of its own.

The Adjudicator didn't appear to notice anything untoward. Instead, he gestured over the map, and the central viewing point flew to the castle of the Swords, growing larger to show the villages dotted around it. There was one larger than the rest, a little town that lay due south on the banks of a river. The Adjudicator tapped it with a bony finger.

"Would you like to take a day trip?" he said. "Perhaps you'd like to learn more about the Swords?"

Ember's heart raced. She cared little for learning about the Swords, but the chance to leave the castle and see more of the kingdom was not a chance she wanted to pass up.

"Yes, please," she said.

The Adjudicator smiled his creepy little smile. "I like it when you say 'please'."

# CHAPTER 11

It was a few days before the Adjudicator sent for her, days in which she paced around her room, chafing at her self-imposed confinement, not wanting to go out into the castle and potentially get into more trouble. As soon as he did, however, she was down in the courtyard early in the morning, waiting for the carriage he'd promised. Gelen packed a bag for her trip, which included a wrapped parcel of snacks and some gold coins in a black velvet pouch. He very much gave the impression of a busy father sending his daughter off to school with her schoolbag and lunch box, and she couldn't help grinning as he gave her a warning about not talking to strangers.

He was going with her of course, along with several guards, and she had imagined that they would travel unobtrusively so as not to draw too much attention to themselves, but it seemed the Adjudicator had other plans. It was bad enough when a massive gold carriage rattled over the cobbles, with crossed sword flags fluttering at each corner and footmen in spotless gold livery settled fore and aft, but it was the sight of the beings pulling the carriage that made her heart sink.

Centaurs. Six centaurs harnessed to the carriage in gold trappings, as though they were ordinary horses. All of them had fresh lash marks across their chests and backs, bloodied red against their glossy hides. It was obvious by their wounds it had been a bitter struggle to get them harnessed, and even though they were eventually bound, there was no submission in their eyes. They were all resentful, cold, alert.

She took all this in with one horrified glance and a dismayed cry escaped her. She went forward, her hand reaching out to take the nearest bridle and tear it off, but a swirl of red, like the flash of a spinning tornado, blocked her path and the Adjudicator appeared. Ignoring her distress—either he didn't notice, or he didn't care—he said, "The carriage will take you directly to Riverburn. Take in the sights, enjoy yourself."

He uttered this last with a curled lip, as if he were sure it would be a quick journey. The coachman leapt down from the box seat in front and opened the carriage door wide to reveal plump cushions in gold and red.

"My apologies," said Ember, carefully not looking at the centaurs. "I'm afraid I can't travel like this. I'm ... allergic." And she sniffed and rubbed her nose as if to prevent a sneeze. "It's the centaurs. And the dust they'll kick up. I'll be a streaming mess any moment."

She coughed, squinted, tried to force a tear.

A frown crossed the Adjudicator's face, but he said genially enough, "I'm not surprised. Filthy beasts."

The centaurs made no reaction to this, their expressionless faces giving nothing away, but Ember felt her face grow hot, her hands fisting at her sides. If she could just punch that despicable jerk right in his revolting face ...

Gelen gave a delicate cough, his gaze on the ground in a submissive servant's pose. "Perhaps my lady might like to take the barge? It's a faster trip by river, and you may find it more comfortable."

"That sounds lovely," she said, quickly. "What a good idea."

The Adjudicator shrugged. "Whatever pleases you."

He jerked his head, and the coachman quickly shut the carriage door and returned to his seat. He didn't touch the reins, merely murmured something that sounded more like a polite request than an order, and the centaurs marched forward as one, dragging the carriage away.

Ember peeked up at them through her lashes, catching the eye of a centaur bringing up the rear. He gave her a slight nod. With the Adjudicator's eyes on her, she didn't dare acknowledge him, but she hoped the nod meant he knew she was on his side.

"I have kingdom business to attend to," the Adjudicator said, much to Ember's relief, for she'd been afraid he had planned to go with her. "Have a pleasant day, my dear. You're under my protection. None shall harm you."

The consideration he was showing her was unnerving, but she smiled and thanked him prettily, and with a feeling of relief, hastened away with Gelen at her elbow and an accompaniment of guards behind her.

"What was he doing, making centaurs pull the coach?" she hissed as soon as they were out of earshot.

"I'm not sure, my lady." Gelen looked just as distressed as she felt. "It's not usual."

"I'd like to see him try to put Swirl in a harness," she said with bitter amusement.

The corners of Gelen's mouth quirked in wry agreement. "He'd not like that."

The outer buildings in the utility part of the castle were busy, and on any other day, she might have felt compelled to linger. The forge was hectic with fire and acrid smoke and hissing steam as sweating fae pounded metal, the kitchen gardens were bursting with vegetables and herbs, and there were pens with pigs and ducks and other more unfamiliar animals, like the blue-feathered cheenuns, and the docile lizard-like binians, which Ember recognised with a thrill of vague disgust as the glamoured 'chicken' that had graced her plate at the banquet.

Beyond the courtyard, they took one of the wide, meandering grassy paths through the manicured gardens and down to the river. She had last visited this area of the castle grounds during the final match of the tournament, when Cole had forced her to swim for her life. But today, the riverbanks were clear of baying spectators and supporters. Tied at the dock was a beautiful barge in the castle colours of black and gold, a simple pennant with a pair of crossed swords flapping merrily in the light breeze.

The bargeman emerged from the cabin below. He was a portly fellow with a thick mane of golden hair curling over his shoulders, gleaming with a fresh brushing. He barked an order and a couple of deckhands sprang into action, settling a ramp into place so that Ember could board.

"Can't take your escort, I'm afraid," said the bargeman, eyeing her entourage of silent guards in full metal armour, heavy swords at their hips. "Not unless you want to swim there."

"Oh, no, that's fine. Sorry," she added to the guards. "Looks like you're off duty." They hesitated, glancing at one another, and she said tersely, "The Adjudicator said I was under his protection, remember? I'll be fine."

The guards stood back as she and Gelen climbed aboard, and she was thankful they wouldn't be dragging at her heels all day through Riverburn. She wanted to blend in with the locals, a feat which was hardly likely with an army tagging behind her.

She settled at the edge of the barge as the captain cast off. The deckhands wielded long poles, pushing the boat away from the bank and into the flow of the river. Ember waved at nothing in particular, her heart lifting, as the distant castle grew smaller and smaller.

# CHAPTER 12

S he remained on deck for the entire journey, leaning over the rail to contemplate the countryside, giving Gelen permission to take a deckchair nearby. Within minutes, he was asleep. Ember could hardly blame him; the current was gentle, and the barge drifted along with a soft undulation that made her feel more relaxed than she'd been since she arrived.

She kept a wary eye out for the naiads, fierce creatures that lived in the depths, with long hair and flesh wrapped in rough sharkskin clothing, but there weren't any. Instead, she saw schools of tiny glassy fishlike creatures with wings on their backs instead of fins, flying out of the water to hover on the surface in groups, before splashing back again in a synchronised wave. Occasionally she glimpsed wild water sprites swimming beneath the surface, human sized and beautiful, with eyes so eloquent that Ember fancied she understood them without a word being spoken.

"Don't look at them too long," said the bargeman with a grunt. "If they know they've got your attention, they'll come up and sing at you, and then you'll be in trouble."

Ember raised an eyebrow, amused. "What can singing do?"

"They'll wrap their little tune around you like a rope and then tug on it. You'll dive right in, and you won't even care, not even while you're struggling for your last breath. And then … and then …" the bargeman's voice dropped to a whisper, and Ember leaned closer, "they'll *eat* you," he finished with a roar, and grabbed her arm.

Ember cried out in delighted shock, and the bargeman bellowed with laughter.

Gelen was on his feet in a moment, pushing Ember behind him, and the bargeman raised his hands in apology. "Now, now," he said. "Just a joke."

"It's fine," she reassured both of them, and Gelen went back to his chair, although this time he kept his eyes open.

"New to the kingdom, are ye?" the bargeman said chattily. "Don't have sprites where you're from?"

"No, not at all." She hadn't realised that her outfit and hair had set her so apart. The women in the castle preferred to wear floaty dresses, elaborate updos, and plenty of jewels, and from what she'd seen so far of the little villages they passed, the country women did too—minus the jewels, of course.

"D'ye have those?" and he pointed at a group of large pink fish leaping up from the water, their gleaming bodies and elongated snouts similar to that of dolphin, but the long spiky whiskers sprouting from their faces decidedly not.

"No," she said. "Aren't they pretty?"

"Taste good too," the bargeman said with relish.

He left to bawl orders at a couple of deckhands, and Ember remained by the rail, turning her attention from the creatures of the deep to the countryside. Grazing livestock munched on knee-high grasses, their pastures fenced with high stone walls to keep out whatever lurked in the occasional pockets of dark green wild forest.

They passed villages with thatched cottages and gardens of herbs, vegetables and flowers, with fae out doing their morning chores, hanging up washing, gossiping over fences, tending children. At one house, three male fae were gathered under a tree, staring upward. Perched high in a crosshatching of branches and clinging to the trunk was a very small fae, hardly more than a baby, her pink wings wrapped protectively about her as she bawled her little head off. As the barge went past, Ember caught sight of a sturdy female fae marching toward the scene. She was wiping her hands on her white apron, her wings snapping open in a business-like manner. The men may not have had a clue, but she clearly had it in hand. Ember craned her neck to watch, but the barge slid around a curve and the tableau was lost from sight.

But already, she had an idea for a painting, her mind running riot. A tranquil pastoral scene of gentle colours and fine brushstrokes, and to the side, half-hidden, a moment of movement and action, completely at odds with the setting in which it took place. She turned the idea over, her gaze glazing as the fields and houses slipped past, the view of the countryside suddenly dim and colourless compared to the bright, vibrant world she was creating in her head.

There was a flash of movement from the corner of her eye and she turned to find Gelen setting up an easel with a low table filled with paints and brushes and tools, a pile of canvases in various sizes stacked nearby. She marvelled at that, the way the fae servants always knew what you wanted before you knew you wanted it and smiled at him gratefully. "Thank you."

He nodded to her, pointing out to a small hamlet just beyond the rolling hills. "Greyclare, my lady."

Ember's heart lifted in recognition. Lily's home. It looked just as pretty and placid as all the other villages they had passed. She gazed at the settlement, wondering which house belonged to Lily, and then, as it fell behind, busied herself with her paints.

An hour or so later, she slowly became aware that the river was growing wider and there were other vessels on the water, fishing craft, rowboats, barges like theirs, and bigger boats piled with covered bales and barrels. There were more houses, and buildings too, not as pretty as the country cottages, but more utilitarian, constructed from wood and brick. She left her work, heading to the front of the barge for a better view.

"Riverburn," the captain announced as she reached his side. "We'll be docking at the main wharf soon. You have business there?"

He didn't appear nosy, merely asking as though it was a matter of rote, from a host to a visitor, and she replied easily, "I'm just visiting. Just learning more about the kingdom."

"You'll be heading for the temples, then. The fire pit that holds the treaty is right in the middle. It's quite a sight. Not that you'll be able to see much without burning yourself to a crisp."

He whistled to the deckhands, who sprang into action, wielding poles and digging them in deep to slow the barge and turn it toward the docks. Another threw a rope and a worker on shore caught it and hitched it to a couple of bored-looking mules who twitched their tails irritably as they pulled the boat toward the wharf. The barge was made fast, a ramp lowered, and she stepped ashore with Gelen in tow.

"We return on the current," the captain called out to her. "You've plenty of time."

"Thank you," she called back, although she wasn't entirely sure how long that was going to be. A couple of passersby gazed at her in surprise. She wasn't sure what had attracted their attention, but she knew what kept it. Their eyes were glued to the pendant around her neck and were filled with awe, fear, and resentment.

"They thought you were a soldier," Gelen clarified. "They're not used to ladies in trousers."

"I'm not a lady." She made to tuck the pendant inside her shirt, out of sight, but Gelen stopped her.

"Perhaps it's best you keep it showing. The local fae don't like foreigners, none of them have ever seen a human, and you don't look like them either. Trouble won't be far away. The pendant will keep them clear."

She acquiesced to his warning, but the pendant was like a siren, the flashing orange jewel drawing attention from everyone they passed. At first, she nodded and smiled in acknowledgement, feeling like a marionette bobbing on strings, but as the crowd increased and the weight of their stares became too much, found it easier to ignore them instead.

"Where would you like to go?" said Gelen. "Some refreshment? Shopping?"

"The temples." The words in her mouth gave her a tingle down her spine and an itch between her shoulder blades, as if an insect were burrowing into her. She flexed her shoulders, the tingle passed, and she thought no more about it.

# CHAPTER 13

They walked along an avenue of market carts piled high with various goods that had come off the boats. One end of the wharf smelled decidedly fishier than the other; bins and troughs piled high with freshwater fish, shellfish, and a lurid green river-weed, which must have been a delicacy, for Gelen murmured several outraged comments at the price. The smell lessened the further they moved on, and soon they were in an industrial area, noisy with metal clanging and workers calling to one another, and rank with the sharp smell of sweat, horse, and smoke.

A queue of fae caught Ember's attention, and Gelen muttered, "How now, what's up?"

The nearby forge was busy with perspiring fae, some pumping bellows to make fires blaze higher, while others hammered metal before plunging it red hot and hissing into troughs of water. A table in front of the forge held knives, swords, and helmets, and a sharp-eyed woman was displaying the attributes of each, as well as her own, Ember noted, observing her shirt tied rather loosely at her bust. All the metalware looked to be serviceable, rather than decorative, a far cry from the elegant weapons and armour Ember had seen worn in the castle. Still, she thought, a rough blade could cut just as well as one elaborately wrought.

"Why so many?" Ember asked, gesturing at the queue.

Gelen gave her a pointed look, and Ember fell silent. She had been told often enough that the kingdom was in turmoil without a Sword at the head. She hadn't considered how that would affect the people living here. It appeared they weren't willing to just sit back and wait to see what happened next.

They moved past the forge and into the town proper, with twisting cobbled streets, stone houses and buildings, street lanterns burning with a golden glow even at that late hour of the morning. Fae hurried on errands, many loading up on goods, or pushing carts piled high with household objects.

Gelen's brows drew together in a scowl. "They're either moving on—or preparing for a siege."

He cast a wistful glance behind them, back toward the barge, and Ember, guessing what he was thinking, shook her head. "Oh no. Not yet. We only just got here."

Gelen gave her an exasperated look, but his voice was as courteous as always as he murmured, "Of course, my lady."

To distract him, she asked about the fae wrapping their wings about them as high as they could to avoid their feathers trailing in the dust, and he explained that magic was regulated in built-up areas; it was illegal to fly for fear of accident. It didn't appear that those regulations extended to weapons; many wore armour, and most had daggers or swords at their hips.

The crossed swords sigil was prominent on doors, signs, flags and walls, the severity of the emblem incongruous with the hanging baskets of flowers, pretty gardens, and mosaic-tiled courtyards. Buildings were embossed with metal panels, filigree designs reflecting the light. Ember had to work hard to stop her mouth from dropping. Even with magic strictly regulated, you could still buy magical products from the various shops, and there were everyday items on the streets that were clearly enchanted too: statues fashioned from coloured smoke, mirrors made with ice that never melted, and wooden toys that sang and moved, without need of a mechanism of any kind.

An inn lay up ahead, a sign with crossed swords set over a plate and mug, and on a whim, she said, "Let's get something to eat."

Gelen looked uneasy. He pointed toward an orange glow on the sky that Ember had noticed previously, but with so many other things to take her attention, she hadn't commented on it.

"My lady, the temples lie just yonder. We could be there in a trice and then enjoy refreshment on board the barge."

"Is it not a good place to eat?"

"I've heard they serve a good table," Gelen said slowly.

"Then why can't we go in?"

"We can, my lady. You can do anything you wish."

A group of young male fae were moving toward them. She had almost grown used to the stares, but these fae were staring at her with such open hostility, she was shocked. The whisper of a barbed threat floated to her, and although Gelen's expression didn't change, he moved closer to her, almost herding her to the edge of the pavement away from them. All her senses were on high alert as they passed, but Gelen's whispered assurance, "They'll not touch you. They don't dare," gave her courage.

With more confidence than she felt, she gave them a hard stare as she pushed open the door to the inn, and they averted their eyes and continued on.

Inside, fae crowded upon benches at wooden tables enjoying their midday meal. Gelen spotted an empty booth over on the far side and led the way. The animated conversation and laughter slowly died, and by the time the pair had settled themselves, the room had fallen silent. Ember took a quick, furtive look around at the curious faces, the narrowed stares. Gelen stared resolutely at the tabletop as if he'd found something extremely interesting in the polished grain of the wood. She lifted her chin, not wanting to appear intimidated, not wanting to give anything away at all, and gradually the chatter began again, albeit somewhat muted than it had been previously.

A stout woman in a white apron and russet-coloured wings came over, wiping her hands on her apron. She gave a little curtsey as she reached them. "You'll not mind them, my lady," she said reassuringly. "They're just curious. We don't get many of quality in here."

"I heard the food is good," Ember said with a warm smile, hoping the woman wouldn't spit in their plates the minute she was out of sight in the kitchen. "I'd like some wine and something to eat."

"We've a good game pie, but we don't do wine. We brew our own ale and cider."

"Ale, thanks."

She looked to Gelen, who put up two fingers to indicate he wanted the same, and the woman bustled off. He relaxed back into his seat, but his eyes were still watchful.

Striving for a casual air, Ember gazed around at the crowd, all workers, by the looks of the patched homespun clothing and battered shoes. Most of the fae resembled humans, apart from several sets of wings, but there was a male with horns sprouting from his forehead conversing with a handsome fae clad in soft forest green, out of place in this crowd of browns and grey.

"The Seeds," said Gelen, following her gaze. "The green fabric is a type of flora velvet that grows in the archipelago. Tourists."

Ember smiled. Funny to think of the fae going on holiday.

She stared out the window to escape the sneaking sideways glances, although there wasn't much to see in the inn's tiny brick courtyard. It wasn't long before the woman came back bearing a tray with two thick slices of pie and two mugs of foam topped beer.

"I know you'll eat as fast as you can and be on your way," she said conversationally, giving them both a pointed look as she unloaded the tray.

The grateful smile fell from Ember's face, and she shot Gelen an outraged glance. He made no comment, and the woman took her tray and hurried away.

"Rude." Ember gave the pie a vicious poke with her fork. It certainly smelled delicious, with its flaky brown crust oozing gravy. There weren't any little reptile snouts poking out of it, but she still wasn't sure if it was safe. The woman's hostility had a pleasant veneer, but it had been there all the same.

Gelen carved himself a piece and ate. He swallowed and nodded. "Eat, my Lady. They'll not kill you here. Too many witnesses."

Ember gave a surprised chuckle, and slowly forked the pie into her mouth, before setting to with gusto. It really was delicious, but the unfriendly looks and occasional hissing comment spoiled it a little. Gelen excused himself to the bathroom just before they left, and while he was gone, Ember took out one of the gold coins from the velvet pouch and busied herself with the glamour brush she carried in her sleeve, before leaving the coin on the table as payment. The crossed swords emblem showed upward, and on the other side, instead of the portrait of the last Sword's face, she had drawn her own.

# CHAPTER 14

They left the inn and walked up the street toward the orange glow. The gradient was slight at first, but as the streets grew narrower and the pedestrians fewer, the street slanted more steeply and then the buildings fell away to reveal a bare grassy hill devoid of trees or structures. It loomed high before them, curiously flat on top, as if a giant had stepped on it. A fug of smoke hung thick in the air. It wasn't the familiar, homely smell of wood smoke, or the acidic tang of the forge. This smoke smelled earthy, like spiced tea, and as she breathed it in, the blood sang in her veins, invigorating, powerful.

Impulsively she placed a hand on Gelen's arm. "I've a mind to go on alone. Would you wait for me?"

He reflexively twitched his arm away and then, as if realising he may have appeared rude, said hastily, "Of course. But do you think that's wise?"

She shrugged. "I don't know."

Without waiting for a reply, she left him there and continued on. The pavement soon petered out into a rutted path through the grass, and she was grateful for the sturdy boots on her feet instead of the soft slippers of lace and satin she used to wear.

The cloud of smoke enveloped her well before she reached the crest. As the hill flatted out, the track split in two, circling left and right around the summit. Now that she was closer to the top, she could see flames and sparks leaping from the crater, from what she assumed was the firepit that held the Treaty of Swords. Heat enveloped her, bringing a sheen of sweat to her upper lip, and she wished she were wearing something without sleeves.

Left was as good a direction as any, but after only a few paces, she flinched in surprise as a building reared up out of the gloom beside her. It was perhaps three stories tall, wide and squat, with white columns and vast steps leading up to an immense door over which was etched the symbol of a curling fern frond.

This must be the temple of the Kingdom of Seeds. She studied it, wondering if she should dare walk up those grand steps and try the door, but the smoke billowed, concealing it from view, and when the smoke cleared, it was gone. After a moment, she carried on walking.

Another building emerged from the smoke, similar to the first, but with slight differences in size and style: arched windows, a tall spire, a ramp instead of stairs. The emblem over the door was a sweeping pair of wings—the Kingdom of Skies.

She continued walking around the summit, passing the temple of Stones and then the Sands, and then came three wide steps leading up to absolutely nothing. This had to be the lost Kingdom of Shields, defeated in battle by the Swords, long ago.

She stood there for a long moment, looking at the bare steps so forlorn, and felt a disconcerting wave of dizziness. Blood thundered in her ears, and her heartbeat quickened. She sucked in two or three deep breaths in an attempt to steady herself, wondering if she were about to faint. Out of the eddying drifts, another building emerged, or rather—the shadow of a building, barely discernible, as though a cautious hand had sketched, and then erased it. Four wide columns supported a sweeping roof, and over the door was a shield, displaying the emblem of a pine tree over three shining beads.

Ember blinked, and the vision faded. The smoke and heat made her feel woozy and she wobbled, stumbling over a loose clod of earth. She twisted, flinging her arms out so she wouldn't crack her skull on the ground, but a muscular arm arrested her fall, drawing her upright as though she weighed nothing, and the harsh heat from the pit became a steady, warm glow. A pair of dark eyes gazed down at her and in that moment, she found herself entranced, as though she were a snake beguiled by a flute-wielding charmer.

She blinked, breaking the spell. "Your Highness," she said faintly, hoping Ashe wouldn't hear the tremble in her voice. The last time she'd seen him was at the dinner when he'd taken her side against Cole, but she wasn't entirely sure if that was to defend her, or merely to needle his cousin.

Ashe made sure she was steady before he released her and she felt a brief sensation of cold as he moved away from her, his cloak billowing like the clouds of smoke around them.

"Have you come to see the treaty?" Ashe said. "I'm afraid you're not mentioned in it."

The barbed comment immediately raised her hackles, and she adopted an aloof air. "Perhaps the Adjudicator could have me written in."

"It's possible. You certainly seem to have him wrapped around your little finger."

She gave a bark of laughter. "Hardly. Besides, he's too ancient to be so pliable. He'd snap."

A slow smile teased the edge of his mouth, but he didn't commit to it, and it faded quickly.

"Why are you here?" she said.

He looked surprised, as though she'd said something impolite. "I'm visiting the temple. Paying my respects to my ancestors. Wishing for better days."

*Praying*, she would have said, although she knew the fae didn't believe in deities higher than themselves. It wasn't in their nature. "The townsfolk seem ... unsettled. They're arming themselves. Some look like they're packing up and leaving altogether."

"Bad news travels fast. Without a Sword, the country is vulnerable to attack from other kingdoms." He gave her a hard look, and she raised her hands in surrender.

"Don't start. I had no choice. You can blame me all you like, but the fact is ..."

He crossed ground in three quick strides, taking her by the shoulders and giving her a sharp shake. "The fact is, we need a new Sword. I know it. You know it. And now the common folk know it too. So perhaps you could tell your new best friend to stop stalling and announce the new contest."

She tried to pull away, but his fingers were biting into her flesh. "Let me go!"

Without waiting for him to comply, she stomped down on his foot and wrenched his pinkie fingers back—a trick learned from her self-defence classes. Leisurely, his hands fell away as if her attack were nothing more than the buzz of an annoying fly, although his expression was grudgingly admiring.

She stepped back, out of his reach. "He said he was working on it." Although, she had to admit, how hard could event organisation be if everything could be arranged with the wave of a hand?

Ashe rolled his eyes. "Perhaps the Adjudicator enjoys being in charge of the kingdom. Perhaps it would benefit him to stall for as long as possible? What if he never announces a new contest?"

As if by reflex, she touched the pendant around her neck and was perversely gratified when his gaze darkened, and he turned away. Sparks rose high from the pit, so high she fancied she saw them streaking across the sky. Or no—they were birds, beautiful red birds with glittering sparks falling from their wings as they flew.

"He would rule with you as his pretty little figurehead."

She could hardly hear him now that his back was turned, the roar of the flames muffling his words but not their bitter tone.

"Why wouldn't I rule?" she said. She didn't know why she was provoking him like this, but she knew it made her angry when he turned his back on her. "I have the pendant. I have the Blade."

"You're not fae and you don't know how to wield him. You have no power except that which the fae give you. They see the Blade with you, and they think you know how to use it. You don't."

He spoke with such conviction she almost believed him. And yet, she thought, Tana *had* obeyed her when she'd wanted to return to Earth, had helped her travel through the veil. And he had put up a barrier between her and Cole, had burned him and flung him away. She may not know exactly what she was doing or how to do it, but the

Adjudicator was right—Tana the Blade had bonded with her, and she *could* use him, sort of, even if Ashe disagreed.

"And if you can't use the power of the Blade, then the kingdom is vulnerable to any other kingdom who might want to swoop in and take it." He jabbed a finger toward the empty space where she'd seen the shadow of the Shields temple. "That's what happened to the Shields, and I'll be damned if it happens to the Swords. You tell the Adjudicator he needs to get a move on, because if we go down, he does too, and so does your own world, no matter whether or not you believe it."

He glared at her, his dark eyes so full of loathing that she flinched in dismay, reminded of Cole at his most vicious. But there was none of the twisted longing that Cole emanated, none of the push-pull of desire and hatred. Ashe's glare was just pure animosity, and it sent a shaft of fear through her.

She turned and walked away, resisting the urge to run for her life. The gusts of smoke soon filled the space between them, and when she stole a glance back over her shoulder, he was gone.

# CHAPTER 15

E mber didn't bother trying to find the Temple of Swords in the fog. She merely kept her eyes on the track as she hastened down the hill, trying not to stumble on the rough path, trying to forget the look of fury in Ashe's eyes. He'd never looked at her like that before, and she didn't like it.

Gelen was waiting where she had left him, his anxious countenance clearing as she approached.

"Did you enjoy that, my lady?" he asked, falling into step with her.

"If this was my world, there'd be tourists everywhere, and carts selling programmes and souvenirs and food and tee-shirts. I'd probably buy a little fridge magnet," she told him, and he widened his eyes in both disbelief and confusion. "It was quite strange. Peaceful. I didn't go inside the temples. I just walked along the path."

"I'm not sure if you'd be permitted to go inside, being a human and all ..." he broke off, clearly discomforted that his comments might be misconstrued as rude. "I mean—you hold the Blade, so maybe that would have made the difference."

She shook her head, suddenly weary. "I didn't go inside. It doesn't matter." She frowned as a thought occurred to her. "Gelen, the symbol of the Shields is a pine tree and beads. Why is that?"

"For the resin, my lady. They used it for decoration and jewellery and such. It was quite important to them."

She thought about that as they moved down the hill. She'd once painted a picture of the Shields column in Alena's forest and had imagined a pine tree as their motif because the actual column was in ruins, and she didn't know for sure what it was. How strange she had been correct.

They moved back through the town, taking their time, visiting a few shops. Ember bought herself a finely made dagger from a metalworker, and bought Gelen one too, which he accepted with some surprise, turning it over in his hands in appreciation before thrusting it into his belt.

Eventually, they headed back to the barge where the captain was waiting for them. There was a strong whiff of spirits about him as he helped Ember on board, and he certainly seemed rather jovial as he bawled for the deckhands to untie the ropes. Ember had a hazy idea that mules on the towpath would drag the barge upriver—the boat had no engine or oars to pull against the current—but to her surprise, the current had switched direction, and they were lazily floating along with the rush of water again, back toward the castle.

She stayed up on deck for a time, but the glare of afternoon sunlight hitting the water made her feel queasy and so she went below. The passenger cabin was a plush affair with a rolled arm sofa and a cunning hammock made with a silky-smooth woven fibre that Gelen informed her was spider's webbing. The spiders in the kingdom were terrifying creatures, and Ember abruptly ceased stroking the hammock and shuddered, thankful they weren't making an overnight trip.

Gelen left her reclined on the sofa and went above. She lay there for a few minutes, her arm over her eyes for she was sure a headache was about to come on, when she felt the barge shudder, as though it had nudged an outcrop of rocks before slowly moving on again.

She opened one eye, wondering if she should leap to her feet and search for a lifejacket, when the door swung open. Ashe stood in the doorway, looking entirely too large for the small room.

"Your Highness!" She sat up, flustered, hoping fervently he wasn't there to blast her into oblivion, and deciding she'd better just play it cool. "Are we giving you a lift?"

He raised his eyebrows at that, and she rephrased it into language he would better understand. "I mean, you're coming back to the castle with us?"

"I came to apologise."

She blinked, wondering if she'd heard correctly.

"I spoke out of turn with you earlier. I should not have."

She didn't know how to respond to that, and there was a confused silence before she finally said, "You said what you thought. I'd rather that—honesty—than words disguised in other words. If you know what I mean."

He was still hovering in the doorway and she invited him to enter, but there was nowhere for him to sit, and he stood in the centre of the room until she hesitantly patted the seat next to her. The sofa was small enough that their elbows were practically touching and again she felt his scent creep over her, a delicious concoction of spices and honey, tinged with an inimitable layer of magical power. To her consternation, she found she was leaning in toward him, as if hoping for his touch. She hastily sat back before he noticed. She had no wish to get entangled in another ill-conceived relationship. She didn't need a man in her life, much less a powerful fae. Still, he was gorgeous, though.

He didn't seem aware of the thoughts racing through her head. He was merely staring straight ahead into space. Eventually, he broke the silence. "They say it was truly terrible. The last war, with all of Esha torn apart, and the Shields burned."

His remark caught her by surprise, and she felt a strange twinge deep inside at the mention of the Shields. The temple came floating into her mind, a ghostly imprint appearing out of the smoke before fading away to nothing.

"It took years for Esha to settle back into a harmonious whole again. But the fate of the Shields is an unspeakable reminder of what happened. We cannot allow it to happen again. The Seeds have always wanted to extend their territory. The Sands egg them on for fear the Seeds will turn on them instead. And although you have the Blade, you don't have power or support. You cannot hold our kingdom."

"If Cole rules, it'll be worse than me," she said acerbically. "You know that."

"If I lose and become the Blade, I'll still have more influence over him than I do now. And you never know ..."

His voice trailed off, but she finished his sentence for him. "You might win."

"Yes."

A thought had been niggling at her for some time now and she ventured, "Ashe, if the war was as bad as you say, what happened to Earth?"

She had always been told that Earth's fortunes were connected to fae. If the Swords were in turmoil, Earth's temperatures rose. If the Seeds fought, disease and pestilence followed. A fae civil war should have thrown her world into chaos, and yet there was nothing in her living memory of such a destructive event.

"And here lies the power of the Adjudicator," he replied. "He and his counterpart ..."

"There's another one!"

"There *was*," Ashe corrected. "They had a plan to manipulate time. It wasn't easy. They had to enlist an army of fae to help strengthen their magic, and they acted as conduits to cast the war back in time, otherwise you'd all be ..."

"Exploded to dust," she finished.

He gave her a quick, surprised smile, one that showed the glint of white teeth. "If you like. They saved humankind, but the dinosaurs ..."

She gave a surprised chuckle. "No. Seriously?"

He frowned. "I am serious."

"I mean, it's terrible, of course, but really? It wasn't a comet?"

"Well, it was. Of sorts."

She fell silent, running her fingers restlessly through her hair. "Okay. I get it. War is bad, Earth is doomed."

"Cole and I could have this done in an hour, but the Adjudicator delays. Why?"

"Nothing to do with me, I swear. I don't actually want to be here. I have a life, you know."

"I know." Unexpectedly, his eyes grew warm. "Your new life suits you. You look ..."

She flushed as his gaze raked her from top to toe. "Not so frilly."

"Not so frilly," he echoed.

There was silence, but this time it wasn't uncomfortable or awkward. "Would you ... would you like some wine?" she offered, not wanting this new, pleasant camaraderie to end. She hadn't really talked with anyone since she arrived. Gelen's one-word answers and decided lack of enthusiasm for friendship didn't count.

As if on cue, the door opened and Gelen entered, carrying a bottle of wine beaded with condensation, and a single glass. When he saw Ashe sitting on the couch next to Ember, he flushed to the roots of his hair and bowed clumsily, only just saving the wine before it toppled to the floor. He placed the wine on the table and scuttled out, returning almost instantly with another glass and a silver tray piled high with little dainties, cakes, sweets, breads, and dips. He poured the wine, and then beat a hasty retreat, giving Ember a wide-eyed glance as he closed the door. Ember wasn't sure if Ashe had noticed Gelen's awkward behaviour; he hadn't acted as though he'd even seen Gelen at all.

They clinked glasses together and sipped. He smiled at her over the rim of his glass, and she felt heat blossom deep in her belly.

As they ate, they talked, lightly, about Riverburn and the temples. She showed him her new dagger and mentioned she had purchased one for Gelen as a gift. A tiny frown creased his brow at that, not in condemnation but in surprise, as though he couldn't quite believe she would do that for a mere servant.

"You don't approve of me buying him a present?" she teased.

"To be honest, I'm astounded you even know his name."

"Don't you know the names of your servants?"

He shook his head. "They change. As soon as I get used to one, another pops up in their place. My housekeeper, Milan, keeps them in order. She's been in service to me since I was small."

"Then it's Milan who ensures you never get to know your staff," Ember said. "I wonder why?"

He frowned at that, and fell silent, considering her words.

There came a rustling at the open window, and she started in shock, slopping her wine on the floor. A crimson bird stood on the sill, blazing hot to look at, with two red plumes rising from its crest, and sparks floating all around it. It hopped inside, flew to the table, and let out a melodious squawk.

"My goodness!" Ember cried. "How do we get it out? Shoo! Shoo! It'll burn the table." She flapped her hand ineffectually at the bird, who merely arched a graceful neck.

"It's a firebird. It isn't hot, though. You can touch it." Ashe leaned forward and unclipped a small brown cylinder from the bird's leg. He removed the cap, and a piece of parchment fell into his hand.

"A messenger. Clever." Ember raised a hand to stroke the shiny red back, and then drew back, still wary of the sparks swirling about its feathers like dust motes in a ray of sunshine.

Ashe gave a surprised grunt, and she looked at him. "What does it say?"

"It's from the ruler of the Kingdom of Stones," Ashe said. "He's inviting you for a visit."

# CHAPTER 16

E mber had met Sten, the ruler of the Stones, a handful of times during the tournament, but she hadn't yet met his ruling counterpart. He disliked Cole and took a perverse pleasure in annoying him, offering to take Ember off his hands more than once. He had a caring, grandfatherly air about him, reinforced by his grizzled beard and slightly cynical air, but she had no real idea how old he was, or how old any of the fae were, for that matter. "How did he know I was here?"

"Sometimes he can read the future in the stones. They're polished crystals, carved with symbols," he clarified at Ember's confused expression. "The symbols tell him things. Perhaps they told him you were here."

"Or perhaps it was the firebirds that flew over us at the pit?" she said, thinking back to the flock of red birds and their trail of glittering sparks.

Ashe laughed. "Yes, that's more likely. He keeps them as spies. He's never dared to send them into the kingdom before, but it's easier now, without ..."

She held up a hand. "Don't say it."

Without a Sword, he meant. It always came back to that.

"Will you tell Sten I'd love to come?" she said to the firebird, and it cocked its head, as if in confusion.

"It's not as easy as that. You're the ... well, I'm not sure what you are exactly. The keeper of the pendant, I suppose, which means this would be a diplomatic mission, from one kingdom to another. The entire event needs to be managed, orchestrated, gifts prepared, speeches written, entourage chosen ... it could take weeks."

"Weeks?" Ember wrinkled her nose. Why did everything in Esha take forever?

"The Adjudicator will want to be a part of it," Ashe warned her. "The Stones are powerful. They've always been our allies, but they could also prove to be extremely formidable enemies."

"It's just a visit," Ember argued. "And if Sten wanted it to be a big formal thing, wouldn't he have sent a big formal invitation with parades and trumpets and things instead of a parrot?"

Ashe considered this and shrugged. "If we are to visit, we should do so as quietly as possible."

"We?"

"Of course. You cannot go alone. You, as a hostage, would be very tempting." His gaze drifted slowly to her mouth as he said this, and then he turned his attention back to the firebird, replacing the cylinder on its leg. "I have power enough to protect you if need be."

She was glad he had turned away, that he couldn't see her face. She was struggling to control the frisson of excitement that had bloomed deep within her at the word 'hostage' and the way he had leisurely studied her mouth, as though he had been wondering what those moist lips and clever tongue might do. All at once, she recalled nights of sensual submission to a will greater than her own, and she found herself wondering if Ashe liked to play those games too, and what it would feel like to be his willing slave ...

She bit her lip, forced herself back to the present. Ashe still had his back turned, but his hands were clenched at his sides, his knuckles showing white, as if holding himself back from doing something he might regret.

"We shall come." The words were slithering through his teeth, sibilant and flowing, in a strange rhythm that she knew wasn't her own language, and yet she could discern the meaning behind them as though the words were clouded in haze.

The bird gave a little bow, the two sweeping plumes on its head brushing the tabletop. Ashe made a sharp throwing gesture, as if he were about to hurl a rock at the bird, and in a flash of red flame, it vanished.

"What did you do?" Ember was aghast. It looked as if Ashe had fried the poor thing.

"I sent it on ahead."

Ember gave Ashe with a quizzical look, remembering the map the Adjudicator had shown her. "We take the barge, then? Won't that be a terribly long journey?"

Ashe shook his head. "No. We can't just cross the border. We'll go the proper way. Tell no one. I'll take care of your servant."

"The proper way? Which is ...?" she prompted.

A wisp of black smoke rose from his cloak, coiling about him, and growing thicker until it almost concealed him from view. "I'll meet you back at the castle. In Alena's rooms."

"The forest?" At first she was confused, and then her expression cleared. "The columns?"

There was no reply. The smoke vanished, and he had gone with it, the barge shuddering underfoot with the displacement of his leaving.

Gelen returned to the room shortly afterwards, and as he tidied up, he picked up the two wineglasses with a bemused expression, as though he wasn't sure how they had got there.

"We should be arriving soon, my lady. And I was told ..." His voice faded, and he scratched his head, frowning.

"Yes?"

"Pardon me, my lady. I'm not sure."

Ashe had cast some kind of enchantment on him, she was sure of it, and to test the theory she said, "I won't need your services when we return. I'll call for you when I'm ready."

The old Gelen would be instantly suspicious, might even have protested, but now he just nodded absent-mindedly, saying, "As you wish," and wandered out of the room.

She followed him up on deck, watching the last of the placid scenery slide by until they finally pulled up at the castle dock. It seemed as though everyone on board had felt the effects of Ashe's visit; the captain had fallen silent and barely managed a gruff, "Farewell to ye, missy," and the deckhands made such a mess of the ropes that she had to leap a widening gap from barge to shore. She asked Gelen to return the paintings she had been working on to her room, but she wasn't sure if he had heard her; he still had a dazed look on his face as though he had gone several rounds in a boxing match.

She'd been afraid the Adjudicator might be waiting on shore, but he was nowhere to be seen. There was however, her entourage of guards just as she had left them. She was instantly remorseful for wasting their day, but they didn't show any displeasure at being left on the riverbank for hours. They accompanied her back through the castle grounds, and on to Alena's forest. She left them at the archway, requesting they take the rest of the day off; she could easily get a guide back when she was ready.

Walking alone through the trees, she made a detour past Alena's pool, unable to resist a quick glance at the mirrored surface to check that her hair was relatively tidy. She should have had a quick shower, got into fresh clothes, a squirt of perfume perhaps ... but it was too late now. Ashe was already waiting for her in the centre of the columns, a dark shadow against the green.

"Are you ready?"

"You told me once that you had to be fae to use the columns," she reminded him.

"Yes," he agreed. "You do. Anyone else will be crushed into nothing."

She gave him an indignant look, and he laughed. "You have the Blade. It should be fine."

"*Should* be?"

He turned, facing the column with the symbol of a jagged mountain peak carved into it. Laying a hand against the sigil, he muttered under his breath. It wasn't a command, Ember thought, but more like a request. A seam of light flashed, outlining a rectangular doorway and then the light vanished, revealing a dark tunnel in its place.

"Is it far?" she asked.

"Not at all," he replied. "Are you afraid?"

She met his gaze and raised an eyebrow with what she hoped was a nonchalant air. "No."

He stepped through, and she followed him.

# CHAPTER 17

The darkness of the tunnel enfolded around her and whisked her away, flinging her about as though she were a sock in a washing machine. She didn't have enough breath to scream, she couldn't see anything but unrelenting black, and the motion was sickening. It could have been five minutes or five years when she was eventually shoved out of the maelstrom. Her feet finally found purchase on a solid surface, and she sank to her knees and vomited.

Strong hands pulled her to her feet, and she took in a few steadying breaths, wiping her mouth with her sleeve.

"You could have warned me!" she began, but the complaint died on her lips. She and Ashe were standing in a large cavern. Light leaked in from somewhere, illuminating a ring of unsmiling soldiers with sharp pointed lances aimed at them, and four columns looming high next to a familiar pile of rubble. "Sorry," she said into the silence. "Seasick."

There was telltale gleam of amusement in Ashe's eyes, but he turned to one soldier and held out the parchment the firebird had delivered to them. The soldier scrutinised it, nodded, and his companions lowered their spears.

"Welcome to the Kingdom of Stones," the soldier said. "Please follow me."

Ember glanced at the column that had led her in. The doorway had vanished, the sigil of the Stones replaced by the emblem of two crossed swords.

The soldiers closed around them, four ahead and four behind, and escorted them through the rocky cave and into a short tunnel. The air was bracing with a hint of snow on the wind, and when they emerged from the tunnel, she drew in her breath in wonder.

Gone was the placid countryside, sweet villages and patches of wild forest that comprised the Swords' territory. The Kingdom of Stones lay high amongst the mountains. Craggy rocks lined the rocky trail between peaks dusted with snow. A gust of wind skittered past, and she shivered. A careless gesture from Ashe and he was holding a warm black cloak, which she accepted gratefully. She swung it over her shoulders, fastening it at the front with a little brooch with the symbol of the crossed swords. Once she drew the hood over her head, she immediately felt warmer.

She looked back at the cave entrance, fascinated to see that they had emerged from an open mouth. Ancient hands had carved weathered stone to represent the yawning maw of an enormous dragon. High above, two huge rubies sparkled in the cliff face, dragon eyes, looking out onto the mountainous range.

The guards kept a brisk pace, marching them down the rocky slope through a pass. The track didn't look well-used; Ember had to be careful where she put her feet lest she stumble. Pockets of snow dotted with flowers hugged the dark creases of the rocks—snowdaisies, Ashe called them, the symbolic flower of the kingdom, blooming in the harshest of conditions. The walls of the cliff face rose high, showing a thin slice of clear blue sky above, echoing the tramp of footsteps back from the stone. The pass felt claustrophobic, and twice, loose rock fell from the cliff face, smashing onto the track below. The first time it happened, Ember looked up in alarm, wondering if a bigger boulder was about to smash her flat, but there was no danger—unless you counted the soldier with a bow and arrow, and another and another, on ledges high above, their weapons aimed toward the travellers below.

Ashe didn't appear concerned. He walked as easily as if he were taking an afternoon stroll. Still, Ember thought, such ease probably came with the fact that he could wave away an arrow with a flick of his hand, whilst she would probably end up looking like a porcupine.

When they finally emerged from the pass, they came out onto a bluff, and there in front of them stood the palace of the Stones, glowing like a white shell in the clear light, the lustrous marble slabs accented with gold. Four towers stood at each corner, looking as though they had been placed there for graceful symmetry rather than defence.

A lake surrounded the palace on all sides, now a frozen moat in blue and white. The soldiers led them on a circuitous path over the ice where it was stable underfoot. Ember had no doubt that if a stranger attempted to traverse the lake without a guide, the ice would crack and shatter and whoever was attempting the crossing would plunge into the icy depths. It was a theory that was confirmed when they passed several dead fae with broken wings trapped under the ice, faces and hands pressed against the frigid surface as though trying to get out, mouths contorted in a scream. Ember shuddered as they passed, turning away and burying her face into the soft folds of her hood. For all its beauty, this place, like that of the Swords, was a realm of danger and brutality.

The great doors opened with a clamour of chains and creaking of hinges. Once through, they found themselves in a great courtyard surrounded by high marble walls and defended by more archers on walkways. The escorting soldiers wheeled and left them, heading back out onto the ice. The doors were closed and then two fae, winged in gorgeous tones of blue and silver, came forward, smiling and bowing deep.

"The One and Two welcome you. Please come."

Ashe and Ember followed them, Ember whispering, "The one and two?"

"Sten is the One, the king," Ashe said, "And Ruby is the Two, the queen. She is not a subordinate, though. They rule side by side. A dragon selected them to rule. One day, both will die, and then a new One and Two will be chosen."

Ember was fascinated by this, although their passage to rulership wasn't any less strange than the battle of the heirs in the Kingdom of Swords. But still. Chosen by a *dragon?*

The fae escorted Ember and Ashe through a cleverly concealed door and into the halls of the palace. Ember gazed around in wonder, feeling like a tourist. White stone wall panels carved with fantastical creatures, marble floors polished to a high sheen, high ceilings painted with murals of cloudy skies. The overall effect was glacial, and she shivered as she trotted after the fae.

They were shown into a large room with vast open windows that looked out to the mountains. Flurries of snow danced past the open arches, and yet the room was as warm as if it were a sunny day.

Ember and Ashe settled on a chaise under one of the graceful windows, beside a table already laden with refreshments. The fae politely asked if they required anything more, and when Ashe refused, bowed and left.

Ember could barely restrain herself from kneeling on the plush velvet like a child and gazing out at the view. "It's so beautiful!" and then at Ashe's look of amusement, "What's so funny?"

"Nothing." An expression of tenderness came across his face, but it was so fleeting Ember wasn't sure if she had imagined it or not. "You like snow?"

Her eyes widened, and she gestured at the vast scenery that lay all around: the clear, bright light, the snow-capped peaks, the shadowy-blue mountain valleys and gullies that looked as if they had been scooped away by a giant finger. "Snow? That's what all this is to you? Snow?"

"Brrr," he replied with a mock shiver.

She laughed at him. "I wish I could paint it."

"I'm sure I can arrange that," came a voice, and Sten, the ruler of the Kingdom of Stones, entered the room.

# CHAPTER 18

I gnoring Ashe, Sten immediately crossed to Ember, taking her in a warm embrace and giving her a resounding kiss on each cheek. His fur jacket and thick, heavy-soled boots made him appear even larger, and he smelled of bracing air and the wild outdoors.

Ember knew she'd always fascinated him. One look at Cole and he'd seen the terrible predicament she'd been in, offering to steal her away to the Kingdom of Stones. Ember hadn't taken him up on his offer because she wasn't sure what danger she would have put herself into if she had. But now she was here, she reflected that perhaps she should have done so, and then this business with the pendant would never have happened.

Ashe bowed formally to him, acknowledging his position as a ruler, but Sten merely nodded back. Ashe wasn't in charge of anything—yet.

"Welcome to the Stones." He gave Ember an arch smile. "I knew I'd get you here, eventually."

She smiled back, giving a careless shrug, as if to acknowledge the truth of it. His eyes drifted down to the pendant around her neck and then took in her simple clothing. "You look like a guard now. Which may not be a bad thing, considering."

Ember felt Ashe stiffen almost imperceptibly. Sten's eyes widened, and he tilted his head as if listening to something in the distance before chuckling. "My goodness. Ruby is waiting to greet you. Don't tell her I found you already."

He vanished, a gush of chilly air filling the empty space. Before Ember had time to react to his abrupt disappearance, the doors opened and a fae servant entered. He bowed and said, "The One and Two request your presence in the throne room."

Ashe's mouth quirked in amusement, but he said nothing, and he and Ember followed the servant out the door.

The halls they travelled were unlike the formal, chilly reception corridors they'd been through thus far. There were large windows, clipped potted trees, and the occasional open pathway with a view to rooms below. The temperature was balmy, and Ember felt a little too warm under her cloak. She swung it off, tucking it under her arm.

Finally, they came to a massive chamber with marble columns and arches studded with sparkling gems. Two elaborate thrones stood on a dais at the far end. On one, sat Sten, his outdoor clothes replaced with formal robes, a silver crown set somewhat askew on his salt-and-pepper locks, and next to him sat a woman, regal in her bearing, her black hair twisted up beneath a matching silver crown, her dark skin a perfect foil to her rich purple robes.

Next to them, tussling in a large wicker basket, were two ... Ember gasped. Two small *dragons.* They were hissing and baring pointed teeth, their spiked tails thrashing this way and that as they mock-bit at each other and stood on their hind legs, flexing bat-like wings to look larger and more threatening, before collapsing back down again with little puffs of black smoke.

Ember could hardly bear to drag her gaze away, but she forced herself to focus on Ruby as she bade them welcome with a warm smile, using the formal language of the fae court. Sten said a few words too, as though this was the first he had seen them, which amused Ember. Ashe bowed deeply at the end of the ceremonial greetings and after a startled pause, Ember did too, feeling it would be a little difficult to curtsey in trousers.

"So, you're the new ruler of the Swords?" Ruby said genially, the formal part of the proceedings apparently over. "You're prettier than the last one."

Ember let out a surprised laugh, cutting a sly glance at a stony-faced Ashe, and recalling the explanation she had once given Gelen. "More like a caretaker."

"A usurper, so I heard," Ruby said. A mischievous twinkle in her eyes softened the tart observation, and she directed her next words to Ashe. "Come now. Rather her than the other one, surely?"

Sten leaned toward her and muttered something, and she gave an elegant shrug. "Forgive me. I've just been so bored lately. I'm only teasing. Your little escapade has been the most amusing thing to happen in months."

She gestured, and a servant appeared at Ember's elbow with a small gold goblet of something that steamed and frothed. She smelled it gingerly, and the scent of sweet apples filled her nostrils. Cider, then. She took a sip, and the strong alcohol raced through her, warming her from the inside out and bringing a smile to her face. Ashe, too, looked somewhat happier after his first taste, and he immediately handed the goblet back to the servant. Ember held on to hers, though. It tasted good, and she had a sneaky suspicion it had been enchanted to make her feel safe and relaxed—likely the reason Ashe had given it back.

The two leaders rose from their thrones and the four went through a door into a snug sitting room, with couches lined with fur, beautiful rugs on the floor, and a crackling fire in the fireplace. Outside, the mountains appeared as though drawn against the sky, and a flock of birds flew past that Ember immediately recognised as firebirds. The view was so enchanting that she felt that familiar tingle in her fingers, the urge to paint and create, and she wondered if she might come back some day and capture that glorious view so that she didn't lose it.

Ruby arranged herself on the couch with Sten next to her, and on the opposite side, Ashe and Ember did the same. The door creaked open and in came the two dragons, snuffing the air and making funny little mewing sounds.

"Oh no," Ruby said. "Send them out. They're entirely too distracting."

"They're wonderful," said Ember.

At the sound of her voice, the dragons whirled around and fixed their eyes on her. One rose onto its hind legs, cocking its head to one side. Ember shifted uneasily. They were small, barely knee high, but she imagined that those needle-like teeth might still rip her face off if they had a mind to. The dragon darted to her in a flash of green and before Ember could move, its front feet were on her knee, and it was gazing up at her with chartreuse eyes. It opened its mouth, coughing a little puff of black smoke, and she flinched.

"Try scratching him between his horns," Ruby said. "Don't worry, I think he likes you."

Gingerly, Ember reached out and did as she was bid. The dragon's scales felt slick under her fingers, and the dragon arched its neck, apparently liking her touch.

"He's taken to you," said Sten. A shadow clouded his eyes, one of confusion. He quickly concealed it with a bland smile, but Ember had already seen it, and she wondered why. "Pengrine and Tryth, they're called," he continued.

Ashe let out an amused snort. "It's a legend," he explained, at Ember's quizzical expression. "Two tyrants from the Kingdom of Skies, long ago."

"We hatch them in the nursery and keep them until they're jetting pure fire. Then we release them," Sten said. "They retain memories of us even when they're fully adult, so they think of us as family, of sorts. At any rate, none of them have tried to burn the palace down."

"Yet," interjected Ruby.

"Release day is always a big celebration. When they take to the skies unleashed for the first time and they realise they're free ... it's a marvellous thing."

"Mostly," said Ruby. "Remember Hyza? She refused to go, and in the end, we had to sedate her and take her into the mountains, far away from the palace. Her trainer had to live out there in a cave for a year until she could be bothered fending for herself. But she's given us three of her babies now."

Ruby called for a servant, and one came at once, scooping up the dragons and bundling them into a cage before withdrawing. Ember was sad to see them go; she could have happily talked about dragons for hours, but she sensed this was something more than just a courtesy visit from one leader to another.

Ashe confirmed it with a terse, "Your invitation was unexpected."

"And why should we not welcome the caretaker of the Swords?" Ruby inquired. "It's good manners, surely."

Sten gave her an exasperated look. "We've learned that your cousin has been in conversation with the Seeds. Our friends of the forest have a hankering to expand into the grasslands."

"The Seeds have been wanting that for an age," Ashe said lazily. "Nothing has changed."

"Except that Cole has promised his support if he becomes Sword. If they can tip the Sands too, they will have more than enough to overturn the covenant."

Ember frowned, thinking back to the map that the Adjudicator had shown her. "The grasslands are where the centaurs live."

Ashe nodded. "It's a free state."

"They have no magic, they have no power," said Ruby dismissively. "That doesn't sound like freedom to me."

"That's not quite right," Sten said. "Their magic is different to ours, is all. Theirs is more ..."

"Fortune telling," said Ruby dismissively. "Forecasting and star reading. The Stones can do that."

"Not quite like they," Sten murmured.

"Still not exactly helpful against an army of fae."

"No one can overturn the covenant. It's enshrined in law," Ashe said.

"Laws can be changed," Ember observed. "They do it all the time back home. Mostly to protect big business." There was a brief pause in the conversation as all turned to her in confusion, and she flushed. "Never mind."

"Only death can change our laws," said Sten. "A good many centaurs would have to die for that to happen. And with the Seeds and Sands united, and the Swords on the brink ..." he gave an eloquent shrug.

Ashe gave a heavy sigh. "Then I pledge to you now that if I rule the Swords, the Free Grasslands shall remain free."

"Excellent!" said Sten heartily. "Do you think you could change your cousin's mind, too?"

Ashe shook his head. "I doubt it."

"Small victories," said Ruby, patting Sten's arm. "We'll have to make a diplomatic mission to the Sands ourselves."

"It's good of you to want to protect the centaurs," Ember ventured, and the other three exchanged merry glances.

"It's not about the freedom of the centaurs," said Ashe. "It's about the Sands and Seeds gaining power with territory. The more they have, the more they wield."

"Oh." It was disappointing to find the fae were motivated by materialism rather than compassion, and as Ember gazed around at their bright, beautiful faces, she felt as though she'd inadvertently bitten into the rotten part of a ripe peach.

"Another reason for the Adjudicator to hurry with the crowning," Ashe said. "The longer he delays, the more influence Cole will have."

"He's very charismatic, your cousin," Sten remarked. "Pity he's so ..."

He broke off, apparently suddenly aware to whom he was speaking, and Ashe lifted an eyebrow. "So?"

Sten refused to be drawn, and it was Ember who helpfully filled in the gap. "Psycho."

There was an uncomfortable silence, and then Ruby said brightly, "Come. Enough of politics. I think our guests deserve a little entertainment now they're here. The moon will rise full, and the night ball festivities are already underway."

Sten gave her a stern look. "We discussed politics for barely five minutes."

"But we got a lot done in that time!" Ruby protested. "We've met the caretaker, we've bound an heir to an agreement, we've discussed the welfare of the centaurs. We deserve a break."

A servant appeared in the doorway and bowed. "Rooms are prepared for our guests. Would you follow me?"

Ashe shook his head. "I'm afraid we can't stay. We didn't tell anyone we were coming. We'll be missed."

"Oh, please," said Ember, giving Ashe an imploring look. She liked Sten and Ruby, and it was nice being somewhere where people liked her too, or at least, didn't cast disapproving glances at her or mutter under their breath as she passed.

"Then, of course, we must stay." Ashe's tone was bland, but Ember could feel a terse bite to it. He would rather have returned to the Swords, but he wouldn't argue with her about it in front of strangers. She gave him a grateful smile and watched his features imperceptibly soften. Perhaps he wanted to stay too. He just didn't want to show it.

# CHAPTER 19

The room they gave her was a perfect square, with every side showing a different mountain view: a perfect snowy-peaked volcano, a rugged mountain range, a waterfall of ice streaming down a glossy black cliff, and a valley of fir trees with snow gusting and whirling through the branches—the only window where snow fell.

Luxurious brown and black furs covered the bed, and the fireplace was large enough to stand in. A maid showed Ember the bathroom and offered to bring her some clothing for the night ball. She requested something simple, for she had no wish to float around in a frothy dress, but she didn't want to offend the Stones by wearing something unsuitable for the occasion. After taking a hot bath, she was pleasantly surprised to find a suit lying on her bed which looked very similar to what she was already wearing but in a rich jade with a white fur hood, and sturdy fur-lined boots that laced up to her knee—a rather odd choice for a ball, Ember thought.

The maid brought a tray too, with spiced meats and flatbread, and cider to wash it down. She brushed Ember's hair while she ate, and when she'd eaten her fill, the maid painted her face with subtle make-up and a hint of sparkle, accentuating her cheekbones and lips.

When the maid had finished and curtsied herself out, Ember looked at her reflection in the mirror, startled to see that the lines normally creasing her brows in a frown were gone, and she looked ... happy. Life had been such a serious business since she'd escaped from Esha three years ago. She'd had to overcome so much; her distrust of strangers, her instinct to shield herself from harm and keep isolated from others. She'd thrown herself into her career, unwilling to let anything derail her from excelling at her craft. She'd felt older than she was, looked grey and wan. She'd put it down to the black she wore that drained the colour from her face, to bad lighting, to overwork, to tiredness, to the memories that haunted her night and day. And she hadn't really cared how she looked because she'd been focusing on other things. But now, in this place, high above the world, she could see the difference. She seemed lighter. Prettier. Or perhaps, she thought, looking at the goblet in her hand, perhaps it was just the enchanted cider.

There came a knock at the door and in burst a female fae in a pale blue jumpsuit that clung to every inch of her body, showing off dangerous curves. She gave a hasty little curtsey and flew to Ember to embrace her, a broad smile on her face.

"Hallo, hallo! Welcome! Auntie Ruby told me all about you. She said not to bother you, but I was sure you wouldn't mind. You're the very first human I've ever seen." She gave Ember a kiss on each cheek. "They were going to get servants to escort you down, but I volunteered. Are you ready?"

"Yes," Ember said, rather thrown by the effusive greeting.

"Come on, then. It's still early, but that means we can get the best seats. The moon will be up soon."

She took Ember's hand and led her, much as if she were a small child, into the hallway. The two guards on duty at the door bowed smartly as they passed, and she gave each one a blazing smile. She kept up a light-hearted chatter as they walked, but eventually, Ember got a word in and asked for her name.

The young fae gasped. "Oh, my goodness. I'm Apoli, daughter of Walan, Auntie Ruby's brother. I can't believe I didn't tell you that first. I was just so excited."

"It's fine. Although there's not much to be excited about, you know."

"Oh, I disagree! A human! The captor of the pendant, who seduced the prince, and bent the Blade to her will with her beauty, wit, and charm! I've heard three poems about you already."

"Poems?" Ember said, weakly.

"It's so romantic! I heard Tana the Blade was exceptionally good looking." She gave Ember a critical once-over, as if to discover the secret of Tana's attraction, and then chewed her lip. "I like your hair," she said finally, and Ember had to put a hand to her mouth to hide her amusement.

They came to a wide staircase and descended, their footsteps muffled by thick white carpets. "And Ashe, of course. So handsome. I swear, all the Swords' men are absolutely divine. Don't tell Sten I said that," she added hurriedly, and Ember assured her she wouldn't. "I've never been to the Swords' kingdom. I hear it's very green and flat."

"Lots of farmland and forest," Ember concurred. "And the castle is very ..." she paused, not knowing what to say. Compared to this majestic palace, the castle of the Swords was like a brooding wild animal.

"They say it has a mind of its own," Apoli ventured.

Ember nodded. "That's it. A mind of its own."

Fae crowded the entrance courtyard, all dressed warmly for the outdoors, laughing and chattering. They nudged one another as Ember and Apoli passed through, and Apoli smiled widely all around, enjoying the attention. "Excuse me, make way for the human," she called, leading Ember through the throng.

The temperature difference between the palace and the outside was considerable. The first breath Ember drew cut like glass. She buried her face in her hood as they picked their way along a grit-covered path through a garden blanketed in thick snow. Icicles hung from every branch, glittering in the afternoon light, interspersed with lanterns that would presumably glow bright after dark.

"Is the ballroom separate from the palace?" Ember asked as they walked.

"Oh no. The night ball isn't held in the ballroom. Although," Apoli mused, "That would probably make more sense. No, we have it down at the lake. You'll see."

They came out of the garden onto the banks of a frozen lake, a perfect circle of frosted perfection with a grassy area in the centre for dancing. Music played through the air and skaters were already gliding back and forth, calling to one another and laughing. Above their heads, spots of light glittered, rising and falling like sparks over a fire.

All around the lake were silk-tented pavilions set up with cushions and blankets. Ember followed Apoli along the bank until Apoli found what she judged to be the perfect spot. She laid claim to her chosen pavilion by collapsing elegantly into the cushions and calling for drinks. Much like the palace, the pavilions were decidedly warmer than the outside air. Ember settled beside her and removed her hood, accepting a goblet of cider with relish. She had developed rather a taste for it.

"Do you skate?" Apoli asked.

"Not well," Ember admitted. She'd only been ice-skating a handful of times; the towns and cities where she'd lived enjoyed torrential rain and gale-force winds during the winters, and the experience of ice and snow was new.

"Don't worry, we'll find you some beginner skates," Apoli said, and a servant appeared, handing her two pairs of white leather boots, the blades glittering an icy blue. "Here you go. They won't let you fall."

"I'll be the judge of that," Ember murmured, eyeing the skates with trepidation. Out on the ice, the fae were performing dazzling tricks, pirouetting and leaping, and occasionally a pair of wings would snap out, turning a jump into a slow glide around the lake.

Apoli helped her put her boots on, and then took her hand as she clumped over the snow. Ember gingerly set one foot down on the ice, and then another. To her pleasant surprise, it was as easy as that. The fae boots kept her steady, and soon her confidence grew. Her steps lengthened, her blades cutting sharp and sure.

After making sure Ember wasn't going to faceplant on the ice, Apoli left her and went to skate with some friends, her laughter pealing over the music as she twirled. One of the fae held her close and nuzzled her neck and she kissed him deeply before pushing him away and kissing another who skated at her side. The fae weren't prone to keeping their desires hidden, as evidenced by a few of the pavilions, which were already crowded with half-naked fae kissing and caressing.

Ember continued on around the lake, concentrating on her feet, and then stumbled, wheeling her arms to keep her balance. She'd felt a shift in the atmosphere, a sense that something fundamental, something *elemental,* had changed. The other fae felt it too, for everyone paused in a moment of absolute stillness. As one they turned, watching the newest arrivals make their way through the garden to the gathering: the One, the Two, and behind them, Ashe.

Even at that distance, Ember could sense his difference to the others. Where they were amiable and open, he was aloof, guarded, a looming shadow in black. He scanned the gathering, and then as his eyes met hers, his shoulders relaxed, his tense carriage easing. She gave him a little wave with the tips of her fingers, just to see if he would wave back—had he ever waved at her before? But he merely raised his chin in acknowledgement before bending his head to respond to something that Ruby was saying as they proceeded toward the royal pavilion, more elaborate than the rest, draped in gold. Feeling a little snubbed, Ember turned her back and glided off.

A handsome young fae named Kalin soon joined her. He had slanted blue eyes and an outrageous turn of phrase that had Ember laughing and blushing as he spun her around the ice, and to his credit, had the courtesy not to monopolise her company so she wouldn't feel uncomfortable and crowded.

The sun set quickly, a rosy blush colouring the snowy peaks before the light descended into a dark purple. Lanterns bloomed golden, illuminating the puffs of steam from the skaters' breaths. Music swelled, the tempo growing faster—not the sensual, dynamic music typical of the Swords, but melodies that were more riotous and celebratory. More skaters filled the ice, taking each other by the hand and swinging around in an impromptu, uncoordinated dance. Ember found her hands seized by first one animated group and then another, and she laughed as she whirled, gazing up at the bright flecks of golden light that danced above them, and higher than that, the stars.

She danced until she was gasping for breath, sometimes alone, and once or twice with Kalin, and then skated to the edge, stumbling as she felt the snow under her feet. A servant helped her out of her skates and into her boots, and another pressed a goblet of cider into her hand. A path trodden by many feet wound through the snow, and she made her way along it, past the place that Apoli had claimed, down to the gold pavilion.

She paused at the gauze curtains, giving an awkward bow—when would she ever get the hang of that?—and Sten beckoned her inside. She settled on a cushion, carefully avoiding looking at Ashe seated just across from her.

"You looked like you were having fun out there," said Ruby, who lay sprawled on a pile of furs, bringing to mind a contented cat in front of the fire.

"Magic skates," said Ember. "I would have fallen a thousand times without them." She gazed out at the skaters' revelry for a time and then noticed a white cloud rising into the sky on the far side of the lake. "What's that smoke?"

"Steam," Sten clarified. "If you think the skates are magic, wait until you try the grottos."

"Hot pools," Ashe said, noting Ember's bemused expression. "The minerals are ... invigorating."

"That's one word for it," Ruby murmured, exchanging a coy look with Sten, who waggled his thick eyebrows suggestively.

"I might go and have a look," Ember said. "I haven't had a hot soak in a long time."

"Ashe? Perhaps you'd like to escort Ember?" Ruby suggested, an innocent smile on her face. Her hand sneaked under Sten's blanket, and he jerked upright, giving her a lascivious smile.

"Certainly." Ashe rose smoothly to his feet, holding out a polite hand to help Ember to her feet. Just that brief touch was enough to send a hot fizzle up her arm, and she dropped his hand as soon as she was steady and followed him into the night.

"How long should we stay away for?" Her innocent question was loaded, given the fae stamina for fighting, dancing, and lovemaking. Ashe didn't reply, but she could feel his amusement.

They walked around the lake in silence, Ember careful to avert her gaze from the pavilions. Most had their gauzy curtains drawn, but there was still the occasional glimpse of naked bodies straining together in passion, making her feel strangely breathless.

She caught sight of bright eyes staring at her from a craggy mound. It was a man in a thin grey robe perched in a crouching position, as if he were a rock himself. Even his skin gave the appearance of stone; lumpy and misshapen. His gaze seared her, a burning that arrowed through her chest and to her spine, making the area between her shoulder blades tingle. He looked familiar—or no—not exactly familiar, because she knew she'd never seen him before. It was as if he had babysat her when she was small, before she was old enough to have concrete memories. It was just an impression, and when she blinked, he was looking away as if he hadn't noticed her at all.

"Who's that?" she whispered to Ashe. The man's scant clothing marked him apart from the rest of the fae, who were all bundled warmly in furs, wool, and suede.

"The Stone mage," Ashe replied. "One of their greatest practitioners of the fae arts. Very powerful. His magic comes from deep within the mountains, so I'm told."

She sneaked a look back at the Stone mage, but he had blended in with the rocks so perfectly, she couldn't tell if he was still there or not.

# CHAPTER 20

The clouds of steam grew thicker as they approached the grottos, and tiny beads of moisture clung to the fur of Ember's hood. The first pool they passed was massive, the greenish water simmering with tiny bubbles that slowly floated to the surface before bursting. Twenty silent soldiers surrounded it, facing outward and holding spears. It certainly didn't look very welcoming, and she said as much to Ashe.

"They incubate the dragon eggs in there," Ashe said. "The private pools are further along."

She craned her neck for a glimpse of the eggs as they walked past, and fancied she saw smooth marble shapes in the middle of the pool, but with all the steam, she couldn't be sure.

The path wound between snow-covered bushes, rocky outcrops and trees, and past a cave, the entrance lit by golden candles. Sighs and laughter came from within, and so they carried on, past several more occupied pools, until they found one with a servant waiting outside.

He beckoned them in, and they moved down a candlelit tunnel which eventually opened out into a cavern. Gold flecked rocks in the cave walls twinkled in the candlelight, and a stack of warm towels lay on a bench. The pool in the centre of the cavern was a luminous blue and wreathed in steam. The scent of it wasn't at all sulphuric as she'd been expecting from her experience of hot pools back home, but a clean fresh smell that brought to mind crystal clear mountain streams and windswept hills.

All at once, Ember remembered she didn't have a bathing suit to wear. She'd have to go in her underwear, but she didn't much fancy the thought of soggy undies afterwards.

As if reading her mind, Ashe said, "The servants will take care of you, you only have to ask," and he turned to leave.

"Wait!" Ember said. "Aren't you ... don't you want to come in?"

"I'm not sure that would be wise."

"Don't be silly." She bent and unlaced her boots, hopping a little inelegantly as she kicked them off. "You're on holiday. Live a little."

"Holiday?" He sounded surprised, as if he'd never considered such a thing before.

"Just don't turn around, okay?"

She untied the laces on her jacket and shrugged it off, along with her fleece lined undershirt. A chill breeze rippled across her skin, making her shiver. She dipped a toe into the pool, and immediately warmth crept up her flesh, heating her from the inside as though her blood was simmering in a pot. Goosebumps rose on her arms, but she wasn't entirely sure if that was the frigid air or something else.

She stepped into the water and then sank down onto a stone seat until only her shoulders were above the water. She gave a sigh of contentment. "It's okay. I'm in."

He turned back. "Are you ... feeling well?"

"What do you mean? It's really nice. Come on. I won't look." Dramatically, she covered her eyes with her hand, and then a surge of water lapped at her chin. She dropped her hand to see Ashe, just disappearing under the water.

He came up, water streaming down his face and torso, and she was struck anew by the iridescent colours that swirled almost imperceptibly beneath his brown skin. He wiped his eyes and blinked slowly, like a cat.

"I'd forgotten what this felt like." His voice had taken on a slow drawl, as if he had been drugged. All at once Ruby's offhand comment made sense, and she wondered what kind of effect this magical water was having on him, was having on *her*.

He stared at her, so long that she felt a self-conscious blush creeping up her cheeks, but somehow, she didn't mind. She liked him looking at her like that. It was the first open look he'd ever really given her, unguarded in its sensuality, and she gave him a slow smile back.

"I shouldn't have come in here," he said. "The grottos are famed for their ... seductive qualities."

She could believe it. She felt light-headed, and a heat was building within her that couldn't be attributed to the warmth of the water. Without really being aware of herself, she slowly stood and walked toward him, the water lapping at her hips, steam coiling off her bare flesh. Just to see what he would do, she ran her hands up her body, cupping her breasts, ostensibly concealing them from his view, but at the same time gently brushing her peaked nipples until they hardened under her touch. He didn't move, his eyes taking her all in, and she settled on the ledge next to him.

"This is not a good idea," he said, but his voice sounded as if he didn't quite believe what he was saying. He looked away, as if he were ready to bolt, and then looked back at her with such naked wanting in his eyes that her heart almost stopped.

She took up the unspoken invitation and slipped a hand onto his bare arm. Her heart was pounding in her chest, and suddenly her mind and body were fragmenting with need. She couldn't think of anything else other than his hands stroking her skin, his mouth on hers, and his cock deep inside her. The desire she had firmly locked away since Cole was straining to break free, and she couldn't think of any plausible reason why she should deny it. She leaned forward, her lips a mere millimetre from his, a distance that felt like a vast yawning chasm. She hesitated for a moment, wondering if he was going to pull away, and when he didn't, she kissed him. He froze for only a second, and then his lips were hard on hers, his tongue plunging into her mouth, his hands tangled in her hair. It was just a moment, one hot, wild, freeing moment of lust and passion, and then he pushed her away.

A familiar sensation of cold came over her as he released her, despite the warmth of the water. When she opened her eyes, still half-dazed, he was standing on the side of the pool, already fully dressed.

"I can't do this, Ember," he said, and walked out.

*Fuck,* was all she could think of, and so she said it out loud. "Fuck!"

# Chapter 21

Although Ember didn't feel like bathing anymore, she stayed in the water until the embarrassment and chagrin at being so unceremoniously rejected had faded a little. Eventually she got out, noting that her skin wasn't at all pruney and wrinkly after being in hot water for so long, but smooth, supple, and sweetly scented.

She quickly dressed and hurried out of the cave. The temperature had dropped considerably, and she tucked her hands in her fur lined pockets as she took the path to the pavilions. She had no desire to go back to the royal gold pavilion, where Ruby and Sten were no doubt still entwined, and so she asked a nearby servant if there was a smaller, empty one available, with every intention of crawling inside and sleeping until morning,

The servant led her to a secluded pavilion away from the others, with an unobstructed view of the lake. She sat inside, furs tucked around her, sipping on hot cider, watching the skaters spin and glide. Fae danced on the green in the centre, twirling under a moon which had risen large and silvery white. As the music pulsed and swelled, the dancing grew wilder, more free, and laughter tinkled on the slight breeze like shards of glass. All at once, the sight of Apoli caught Ember's attention. She was dancing on the ice, her blades sending up a spray of powder with every turn, her partner like a shadow, perfectly matching every step she took.

Ember's mouth dropped. It was Ashe.

After she got over the shock of seeing Ashe looking as though he was actually enjoying himself, Ember had to admit he was an excellent dancer. He didn't appear particularly engaged with Apoli though, or perhaps that was only wishful thinking. Still, his expression was polite and composed as she beamed at him, and he kept a distance between them where he could have held her close. They whirled around the ice, fingertips barely touching, and were soon lost in the crowd.

Ember busied herself by tucking the furs carefully around her, although the tent was perfectly warm and her cheeks had grown so hot from chagrin, she wondered if she should just throw herself off a mountain peak and have done with it. What had she been thinking, flinging herself at Ashe? What must he think? Well, it was clear it wasn't what she'd been thinking. How could she have got it so wrong? There had been that strange frisson between them the last time she'd been in the kingdom, although then she'd been so infatuated with Cole, she hadn't recognised it as such. And there was that moment in the cave when he'd kissed her, properly kissed her as though he wanted her too, not just a response out of politeness.

It didn't matter; it didn't matter at all. Look what had happened the last time she'd entangled with a fae. She couldn't let that happen again.

It was cosy in her furs, the beat of the music fading into a rhythm that felt like her own heartbeat. Soon she fell asleep, drifting over the ice on a cloud of steam which buoyed her up over the trees and mountains and down, down, into the heart of a volcano where flames leapt and gyrated, and then she was falling and falling …

A hand on her shoulder shook her awake, and she clawed her way out of sleep with a desperate gasp of air. The flames had been so close. She could almost feel the sparks on her skin. She opened her eyes, finding herself rubbing at her arms as though to rid herself of falling embers. The moon had vanished, and the night was much darker now. Only a few remained on the ice, and Ashe was sitting on a pile of cushions next to her.

"Are you alright?" His dark eyes were concerned. "You were crying out."

"I had a dream. Flames and … I don't know. I can't remember."

The dream had faded, and she rubbed her eyes and yawned. A servant appeared, presenting them with two frothy mugs of something warm and milky that tasted like spicy chocolate. Ember sipped, grateful to be looking at something other than Ashe.

"Look Ember, about before …"

There was something in his tone that made her look up. He looked awkward, his fingers restlessly plucking at the satin edge of a cushion. She didn't think she'd ever seen him look like that before.

"It was my fault. But don't worry, Ashe. It won't happen again." She couldn't help a note of bitterness creep into her tone and tried to conceal it with a careless smile.

"But it wasn't your fault." A frown creased his eyebrows. "That's what the pools are. They heighten sexual arousal. Ruby was just causing mischief. All of Esha knew about you and Cole. I have no doubt she was wondering if the same would happen between you and me, and if she could turn it to her advantage. For all they're our allies, they're our rivals too."

"So that's all it was? Just sex magic?"

He let out an amused snort at that. "I would have thought as a human, you'd be particularly sensitive to its effect. Although ..." A gleam of curiosity came into his eyes.

"Although what?"

"The grottos are ancient, infused with magic that comes from the very heart of the mountains. Fae enjoy their waters as an aphrodisiac and a source of invigoration. Our own magic protects us from the most powerful effects. But you're human. You should have ..."

"Turned into a sex-crazed maniac?" she murmured. "Well, I wasn't far off."

"It could have been much worse. You might have scratched your own skin off to stimulate the sense of touch. You could have tried to tear me apart."

Ember blinked. "Then why the hell did Ruby send me there?"

"She told me to go with you, knowing I could have protected you from the worst of it. Perhaps she just wanted us to have fun."

"Well, I apologise if I made you feel uncomfortable."

"No, you didn't." His voice was quiet, and she peeked up at him over the rim of her cup. "But there's another reason I couldn't—"

She held up a hand to cut him off. She had no wish to hear him say he wasn't attracted to her, that he didn't think of her like that. "You don't have to explain. Why on earth would you want anything to do with me, let alone—do *that*—when you could have someone nice and easy and uncomplicated and fae, like ..."

She looked out over the ice to where Apoli was still dancing, now in the arms of a beautiful female fae with wings that shone silver in the moonlight. "I understand. I do."

"No, you don't." His voice was gruff, and she glanced at him, startled. "Fae appetites are ... overwhelming. We can break humans. You are fragile. But in the same way, humans can break fae too. You've seen Cole, you've seen what he's like now."

She let out a short laugh. "He was always a nightmare."

"He's addicted to you. His time with you changed him, warped him, took him much further from what he was before. Before, he was predictable in his unpredictability. Now he's just dangerous."

"Please don't blame his attitude on me." She could feel her temper rising. "Whatever he is, it's his own doing."

"You—all humans—have a quality that makes us want to possess you. It's just the way you're made." His gaze roamed over her in a fleeting moment of pure hunger, before the shutters came down again, and his expression was as bland as ever.

"Got it," she said shortly. "I'll keep my fragile little hands to myself."

"Then perhaps we might just be friends."

"Friends," she said, thoughtfully. She'd always thought of Ashe as more of an ally, as someone who was against Cole as much as she. Friends was a step up. She liked that idea. "Alright, then. Friends, it is." *Although*, her mind whispered, *friends don't kiss the way you kissed me.*

They sat in silence for a bit, and she felt herself nodding off again. The next time she opened her eyes, the morning light had transformed the snow into a dazzling white and she was alone.

# CHAPTER 22

"I hope you had a lovely time," said Ruby to Ember. Her eyes danced as she added, "I'm afraid the One is still suffering."

"Silence, woman," Sten said. His eyes were bleary, and he looked as though he'd only just woken up.

Ember, Sten, Ruby, Ashe, and several guards and servants stood arrayed in front of the yawning mouth of the cave. The two baby dragons, Pengrine and Tryth, wheeled overhead, giving little smoky yelps of glee, while servants with leather gloves held onto their silver leashes with all their might. That Sten and Ruby had left the palace to escort them to the cave was an honour in itself, even if Sten looked moments away from bending over and vomiting.

"Can't you just magic a hangover away?" asked Ember. If only she'd had that ability during her studies at art school! She would probably have done better in her exams.

"He could, but I won't let him," Ruby said. "The One should be above such things as excessive alcoholic consumption and gluttony. And fornication," she added with a wink.

"I'll do it later, when the witch isn't looking," Sten muttered to Ember as soon as Ruby's attention had turned to Ashe. "Did you have fun?"

"I'll remember it always," Ember said, ducking the question. 'Fun' wasn't exactly how she would have described it.

Sten glanced at Ashe and smiled suggestively. "And did the heir have *fun,* too?"

Ember shook her head emphatically. "We're not like that. We're ... friends. Sort of."

Sten laughed. "Are you sure? I haven't seen Ashe this infatuated since Serafina."

If it hadn't been the mention of Serafina, Ember might have been flattered. As it was, she felt nothing but an unpleasant jolt. Serafina was Ashe's cousin and Cole's sister. The only reason Cole was an heir was because Serafina had taken her own life. Ember hadn't known Serafina meant anything to Ashe beyond the familial. Had Ashe been in love with her?

"Not at all," she replied lightly, but his remark felt sharp like a splinter, and she wished Sten had said nothing.

Ruby and Ashe were still deep in conversation, and Sten put a hand on Ember's shoulder, casually walking her away from the group. He lowered his voice and said, "I wondered if you'd consider coming back for a visit, just on your own?" The puzzlement on her face must have been obvious because he clarified, "Our mage saw you at the ball. He asked about you. It's just professional curiosity; he's never met a human before. What do you say?"

That the Adjudicator or the heirs might consider this an impropriety crossed her mind, but she didn't care. The Adjudicator had said she could come and go as she pleased, hadn't he? Of course, he had likely only meant the castle, but she could choose to interpret his words as she saw fit, just as the fae did when it suited them. "I'd love to. I'm not sure when, though. Things are rather unsettled with the Swords."

As they returned to the group. Ashe shot her a questioning look, which she answered with a bland smile. If Sten had felt the need to ask her in private, it would be prudent to keep his invitation secret.

Ember and Ashe left Sten and Ruby at the entrance of the cave and made their way inside with a handful of guards. Ember had no wish to go back into that frightening darkness that threw her about as if she were a rag doll, but she had no choice. The Kingdom of Stones lay days and days travel overground from the Swords.

They came to the cavern where the columns stood, and from the corner of her eye, Ember caught the flicker of a shadow. She turned just as the collapsed column of Shields reformed itself, the tumbled stones swiftly knitting together, piece by piece, until it stood as high and graceful as all the others. She gaped at it for a moment and then it collapsed in silence. The stones lay as they were previously, a layer of undisturbed dust settled across them as before.

Before she could comment, the rectangular outline set into the column of the Swords blazed, and then the darkness of the doorway beckoned. She hesitated, already feeling her stomach roiling, but Ashe took her hand and tugged her through. Once again, the hideous motion threw her this way and that, and the strange behaviour of the column of Shields flew out of her head. A force thrust her through the black into the forest, and she staggered sideways, just barely keeping the nausea down.

She became conscious that she was still holding onto Ashe's hand, and he was looking down at her, the glossy rainbow of a bubble around them, a bubble through which no one might hear them speak. "Ember, we'll have to keep this quiet. I don't want anyone thinking we're colluding with each other, or that I've made promises to the Stones."

"But the Adjudicator will have to know about Cole plotting with the Seeds. At least it will force him to announce the date of the contest. The longer he delays, the more support Cole will gain."

He released her hand, and she had to fight the urge to grab hold of it again. "It's not your concern."

His demeanour had changed. She could feel it. He was back to the aloof, sardonic Ashe she'd always known, and she stared at him with a vague feeling of disappointment. She'd felt they'd made some kind of progress in their relationship, but perhaps that had only been in her imagination.

"I'll speak with you soon," and both he and the bubble vanished.

She called for a guide, and when the glowing ball of light appeared, she followed it back to her room. Gelen was there waiting for her, showing no curiosity as to where she'd been, merely running the bath that she asked for.

The long soak was welcome, and although it was barely midday, she decided a nap might be in order and ended up sleeping half the day away. When she woke, she felt an urge to paint, and on a whim, discarded the canvas and turned her attention to the bare wall. She would paint a mural, a trompe l'oeil window scene of majestic mountains. She'd paint a window frame to match the real ones in the room, and it would be as though she were looking out at the mountains of the Stones.

Fired up by her idea, she asked for cleaning rags and water to wipe the wall clean before she began, and Gelen, on the verge of apoplectic hysteria at the thought of a lady doing such menial tasks, sent for a band of servants to do it instead. Just to tease him, she took a rag and helped them, ignoring his tuts of disapproval. By the time the cleaning was finished, dusk was falling, and she only had time to pencil in an outline of the window frame before the light grew too dark to see properly. But she was at it again early the next morning, and over the next week, the painting grew and developed, until she had her view of snow-capped mountains and two tiny dragons flying overhead.

She had been so engrossed in her work that she hadn't really paid much attention to what was happening in the palace until one day, as she was considering her mountain scene with a cocked head, wondering if she should add some flowers curling around the painted window frame, there arose such a clamour from the courtyard below that she flew to the real window to look below, Gelen joining her.

A team of centaurs, clad in armour and carrying weapons, called to one another as they marched along the cobbles and headed out toward the rear of the castle. A flag-bearer at the front of the group held aloft a fluttering pennant of green with a gold border that she'd never seen before. A crowd of servants, guards and courtiers watched them go, calling farewells. All looked shocked and upset. Some were openly crying.

"What's happening? Where are they going?" Ember cried.

"They're going home," Gelen replied. "They're going back to the grasslands."

# CHAPTER 23

E mber immediately called for a guide and asked it to take her to Swirl's rooms. She had been there just once before, and only had a hazy idea of how to get there.

The centaur lived in the maze of buildings connecting the castle to the utility areas, which wasn't actually far from Ember's own rooms. The doors of his residence were open a crack, the sounds of grunting and shuffling coming from within, and she knocked once and then twice. A gruff voice bade her enter, and a couple of servants stood aside as she passed, each carrying one end of a heavy, carved chest.

The last time she'd been there, his rooms had been immaculate. Now they lay in disarray: boxes and trunks stacked in a corner, books and papers scattered across tables and the floor. A pile of rubbish lay in a heap next to a roaring fire, waiting for its turn to be cast to the flames. Swirl stood at a table, sorting through a stack of notes, maps and illustrated papers. He looked edgy and tired, but when he saw Ember, he gave her a brief smile, gesturing to a chair. She sat, her fingers fidgeting nervously in her lap; Swirl's aura of unease was catching.

"You're moving out?"

"Cole intends to make war on my home. How can I stay?"

"But if Ashe wins, you won't have to go. I know he'd want good men—I mean, good centaurs—on his side, helping him rule the kingdom, making it a better place."

Swirl gave a rather horsy snort and turned back to his piles of paper, discarding some, tucking others into a leather satchel. "My allegiance was always with his cousin. I doubt the dark prince would have much use for me."

Ember shook her head. "He's not like that."

"There are some who are choosing to stay. They see the economic benefits of our lands being taken and farmed by the fae. Perhaps they prefer the press of the harness telling them what to do, rather than thinking for themselves. Some want a new covenant forged. I cannot allow that."

"If Ashe wins, will you return?" she persisted.

Swirl sighed. He left his papers to stand in front of Ember, placing a finger under her chin and gently upturning her face to the light. She could smell the scent of him, rangy and outdoorsy, a blend of horse and man, exhilarating and yet oddly calming. "Forget about me. Think of yourself. You're under the protection of the Adjudicator, yes? He can withdraw that whenever he wants. The only reason he hasn't prevented the centaurs from leaving is because the covenant prevents him. But he is angry and therefore unpredictable. The country is on the brink of war. As soon as you can, get out of here."

His eyes were intense, boring into hers, the sincerity in his voice making her feel far more alarmed than she had been when the prospect of war was being idly discussed in the Stones' royal sitting room, and for a moment she saw stars alight in his eyes, a galaxy of them, stretching into the vast nothingness of space. She blinked, and the vision was gone.

Swirl dropped his hand and crossed to the other side of the room, unpinning a map of Esha from the wall, and placing it on the table. She rose to join him, and he pointed out the Free Grasslands bordered by the Seeds and Sands.

"The Sands have no need for the grasslands. Their magic comes from the confines of the desert. They're only allying with the Seeds to placate them and prevent them from moving into the Sand's own territories. The Sands might be malleable if they know they have support against the Seeds."

"I know the Stones will work on the Sands to stay out of it," Ember offered. "That might help too."

Swirl glanced at her. "You seem to know an awful lot about it."

"Their rulers invited me to visit, and Ashe came as my escort. Their palace is beautiful. They have dragons, did you know?"

"I've seen the dragons." He shivered, the muscles under his hide rippling like grass in the wind. "One reason I've never lived there. And it's all uphill." He raised an eyebrow. "You and the other heir?"

Ember gave an embarrassed laugh, striving for a casual tone. "Not like that. Just friends. Sort of."

Far from sounding casual, her voice betrayed a plaintive note. She shot Swirl a quick glance, hoping he hadn't noticed, but his attention was on the map. He frowned, brushing his forearm across the map. "Strange."

She peered at the area he had wiped—the grey smudge that signified the Kingdom of Shields. And there, in the middle, the same odd droplet of glossy amber that she had seen on the Adjudicator's map weeks before, except this was larger. Swirl considered it for another moment and then, apparently deciding it was nothing, abruptly rolled the map and slipped it into an open box containing several other rolled parchments.

"That's good," he remarked, as if there had been no break in the conversation. "Look what happened last time."

"That wasn't my fault," she protested. "Cole's a ..."

He gave her a warning glance just as the door swung open again and the two servants returned, one taking down a heavy mirror, the other stooping to lift a couple of boxes.

"It's a pity you won't be able to visit us in the grasslands," he said, raising his voice for the servants' benefit, Ember supposed.

"I'd like to. I could come after the contest of the heirs."

"Anything on two legs won't be welcome down there, especially if the fair heir wins. Best you go home." He waited until the servants had left the room and then said in a lowered tone, "I know you have a friendship with Alena. Ask her if she can help you conceal yourself. I'm not sure why, but you're ..."

"Vulnerable? Fragile? Breakable?" she said sardonically, reeling off all the words she'd heard the fae use about her in the past.

"Different," he said with a wry smile. "There's something in you I can't quite see, not yet."

"Ruby said centaurs can see the future."

"Some of us. The rest work on educated guesses and hunches. And I have a hunch about you, young lady."

That made her laugh. He sounded like one of her old art tutors. She embraced him, unable to prevent a tear from slipping down her cheek. "Be safe."

138

He gave her a rakish grin, shaking back his long mane of hair. "You too."

She left with the guide, hurrying back to her room for a good view over the courtyard. It wasn't long before Swirl passed by, walking with a few other centaurs beside a creaking carriage piled high with belongings, the green flag of the Free Grasslands fluttering merrily on top.

She called out to him and as he looked up, she plucked a rose from her windowsill and threw it down to him. He caught it easily, tucking it into his hair, and with a wave, he cantered off and out of sight.

# CHAPTER 24

Reports of the centaurs' departure from the castle soon filtered out to the surrounding towns and villages of the kingdom and before long, everyone knew the centaurs were returning to the grasslands to prepare for an onslaught on their ancestral rights to their own lands. Other centaurs who had made the kingdom their home joined them, and they took their skills, strength and knowledge with them.

Schools, libraries, and clinics closed, for it was the centaurs who staffed the houses of learning and healing. Townspeople who had once scorned the prospect of war with the delay in the crowning of the Sword, now queued to stock up on rations and weapons with the rest, while those in the country made frantic plans to protect their farmlands and livestock from hungry invaders.

It didn't matter that the Seeds' plans were still only rumour, as yet unconfirmed by a blasé Cole, who confidently strode through the castle halls as if he already wore the crown. The gossip grew and spread, adding tension and disorder to a land already uneasy with the interruption to the tournament and the subsequent theft of the pendant.

Ember, as advised by Swirl, stayed in her rooms, relying on reports from Gelen, who seemed to take a doleful joy in delivering the worst of it, including the rumours there were centaurs imprisoned in the dungeons, accused of treason.

If Ashe had thought that Cole's plotting might spur the Adjudicator into announcing the date of the contest, he was wrong. Day after day passed with no sign to indicate when Ember could go home. Finally, after nearly a month had gone by and she had painted three more window murals onto the stone walls of her chamber, she decided she'd venture out for some fresh air and visit Alena in the forest.

Walking through the hallways lifted her spirits, if only because she had a different view than that of her own room. But she could feel the uneasiness in the courtiers and servants she passed. Voices were hushed, expressions wary, the fae hurrying about with their eyes fixed on the ground, as if avoiding the world around them. Even though a bevy of guards surrounded them, Gelen's hand still hovered over the dagger in his belt, and Ember wrapped her fingers around the hilt of her own dagger, just in case.

Once they reached the forest, she told Gelen and the guards to stay at the archway entrance, and she took the path through the trees to find Alena. The pool that the forest fae habitually occupied shone silver in the soft light, and Ember sank down beside it and gazed at the surface, trying to see through her reflection into the depths below.

There came a rush of water at the edge and Alena arose. She stepped onto the bank and flicked the remaining drops from her fingertips, splashing Ember in the face.

"Apologies," she said, not sounding in the least apologetic. "So you saw it, then?"

Ember was confused. "Saw what?"

"Saw what the heir has done!" Alena's eyes were eloquent with horror. "All those beautiful fae, dead. From beneath the water, I could hear their screams, could feel their lives slipping past me, and I couldn't do anything to save them. His power was formidable in that moment."

Alena was speaking as though continuing the conversation they'd had weeks before, as if no time had passed at all. Apparently sensing Ember's confusion, Alena waved a dismissive hand and turned away, her head bowed. "It was only a moment ago, for me. It will always only be a moment ago, for a long time, I should think. The death of innocents weighs heavy on me."

Ember nodded. "I'm so sorry." She wanted to add, "It's all my fault," because despite what her head told her, her heart insisted everything *was* her fault, all because she'd wanted to go home. The deaths of the fae, Cole's madness, the departure of the centaurs, the Adjudicators wrath, the turmoil of the kingdom, everything. But she didn't. What was the point in stating the obvious?

Instead, she said, "Swirl thought you might help me hide from the fae when I leave. He said I would be in danger once the contest is done and the Adjudicator has withdrawn his protection. Is that possible?"

Alena tilted her head, her emerald hair pins sparkling in the light. "Only if you were here in the castle. The castle has proved to be an ally for you as well."

"But not once I'm back on Earth?"

"No."

Ember chewed her bottom lip, thinking. Living in the castle just wasn't an option, especially if Cole was in charge. The Adjudicator had promised her ten million dollars when she went back to Earth, but even if he wasn't lying and she used it to hire a bevy of bodyguards, she still wouldn't be safe. So where else could she go?

"What about the Kingdom of Stones?"

"What about it?"

"If I lived there. Would it be easier for you to help me there than if I were on Earth?"

A brief frown creased Alena's smooth brow. "Why would you want to live there? The Stones are savages, grubbing about in the rocks with their flying cattle on leashes, stinking carcasses slung across their backs to keep out the bitter cold."

Ember had to laugh at Alena's dismal portrayal of life in the mountains, but of course, Ember had been a guest in the royal palace. The common folk in the villages and highlands would no doubt live a very different life.

"I visited the Stones' rulers. They were really nice. They want me to come back and visit. What's a Stone mage?" she added.

"My goodness, you are full of questions this morning, aren't you? Hasn't anyone ever told you that conversation should flow like a babbling brook over crystal rocks as opposed to the staccato exchange of a merchant haggling with a buyer?"

Ember was too used to Alena's caustic remarks to be offended. "The Stone mage?"

"A powerful magician who has lived an aeon and who draws his power from deep beneath the earth. Why?"

"Sten—the king—wants me to speak with him."

Alena's attention shifted from casual to intent. "Why?"

"I don't know."

Alena gave a slow smile of satisfaction, as if she'd just learned a juicy piece of gossip. "Be careful, my dear. The Stone mage will chisel into your brain—*tap, tap, tap*—and reveal secrets you didn't even know you had."

This comment disconcerted Ember, but she shrugged. "I don't have any secrets."

"Nonsense. Everyone has secrets. Most of us don't even realise we have secrets. Things we've locked away on purpose because they're hurtful. Things our minds have locked away to save us from ourselves. The Stone mage can see everything. Are you sure you're ready for that?"

"I don't know. I suppose so. Why not?" Although she was striving for a casual tone, she felt a strong sense of foreboding at Alena's words. What secrets was she hiding from herself?

"Then when you're done, if you're still in your right mind and haven't been reduced to a drooling mess of lunacy, do come back and tell me about it, won't you?"

# CHAPTER 25

I f she'd thought visiting Alena would give her some relief, she was wrong. Ember's mind raced as she made her way back through the forest. Was it a stupid idea visiting the Stone mage? 'Babbling mess of lunacy' didn't sound particularly appealing. And yet, she was curious to meet him. She remembered the way his eyes had connected with hers at the night ball, as though he'd seen right into the heart of her. What could he discover about her that she didn't already know?

She paused by the Stones' column and ran her hand over the stone, feeling for the seam that outlined the doorway, but the column was smooth with no discernible indentation. So that was it, she thought, returning to the path. She had no way of getting to the mountains unless she were to hijack a carriage, and even then, the Adjudicator would find her within minutes. She could do as she had in the tournament and glamour a pair of wings to fly there, but how long would that take? Likely, forever.

Her mind still going over her conversation with Alena, she slowly became aware that her surroundings were unfamiliar. She must have taken the wrong archway. She stopped at once, looking back over her shoulder, but she had wandered through an intersection of three different halls, and it wasn't immediately clear which one led back to the forest. Candles flickered in the dim hallway, and everything was silent. She was about to call a guide when she heard a shout coming from a window down the hall.

Curious, she stole toward the window and peeked through. The view wasn't of the outdoors, but of a large room with wooden floors and a rack of weapons leaning against a wall. Cole stood in the middle, brandishing a sword with both hands, his forehead beaded with perspiration. It wasn't the sword that Ember usually saw him with, the ceremonial white sword that marked him as an heir, but a regular sword of dull iron.

The floor at his feet glistened with a dark spill of blood, viscous and wet. Opposite, a tall fae wielded a sword, whirling it slowly, his eyes fixed on Cole's hands. As quick as a snake striking, Cole lunged, and the two swords clashed together. The pair disengaged and circled one another, feet placed deliberately, carefully, and then, as if at an invisible signal, the two clashed again.

Now the fighting began in earnest and although Ember was certainly no expert, she thought the other fae was playing more of a defensive game. His attack wasn't as convincing. Perhaps the fae was fearful of hurting the heir, or perhaps he was disinclined to fight for his life. Ember had seen many of Cole's lower servants, their tormented eyes and carefully blank faces incongruous with their grace and otherworldly beauty. Maybe for them, death was better.

Cole lashed out, his sword plunging into the fae's gut and out again with a spurt of red blood. The fae sank to his knees, blood pulsing through his fingers, his head bowed. Ember recoiled in horror, but she couldn't take her eyes off Cole as he strode forward, taking the fae's hair in his hand and jerking the fae's head back with an expression of anticipation and exhilaration on his face. When the fae finally slumped, Cole sighed and stood motionless. He was breathing heavily, and Ember knew it wasn't from the exercise, but something else, something dark and twisted. Finally, Cole snapped his fingers. Two fae servants appeared and carted the body off, careful to avert their eyes from the heir. Cole flexed his hand. A trickle of blood coloured his knuckles. He raised his hand to his mouth and licked at it, delicately, like a cat.

Ember shuddered, clutching the window frame tightly. She felt as if she might faint. When she'd stopped feeling wobbly, she moved back out of sight and whispered for a guide, hoping it would hurry. The sooner she was out of there, the better.

There came the sound of ringing metal, and she couldn't help peeking around the frame once more. Cole had set himself against three fae this time, his sword a blur of motion. It seemed to Ember that they were careful to present themselves one by one, for surely all three at once could have easily overpowered Cole. The first died without a sound, followed by the next. As Cole circled to take the third, he slashed the fae's head right off, and it bounced across the floor, leaving a trail of blood and gore. The empty eyes rested on hers and she gave a cry.

Cole's head whipped up, his eyes boring into hers. In a trice, he had disappeared from the training room and reappeared right beside her. Blood ran the length of the sword, dripping onto the polished floors.

He smiled. "Little stray, you've wandered too far."

Her voice was hardly more than a whisper. "I'm sorry. I got lost."

Out of the corner of her eye, a dancing light beckoned. She backed toward it as Cole moved forward, matching her steps, his pace deliberate and mocking. She spun and ran, but he leapt forward and caught her easily, his hand grasping the back of her neck. He shook her once, twice, as though he were a dog shaking a rat, and she cried out. He thrust her away, and she fell to her knees in front of him, on the verge of hysterical tears. Placing the tip of the bloodied sword blade under her chin, he forced her to raise her head and look at him.

"Your world is spinning closer to ours. Every time the sun rises here, another one of your nations burns. You did that."

It took all she had not to jerk away, for she feared he would cut her throat, no matter what the Adjudicator had decreed. The sword dropped, and he lunged, yanked her up by her hair. It was as though someone had flicked a switch inside her, releasing her from helpless inertia, and she found her voice, shouting at him, slapping at his hands to make him let go. She kicked out, connecting sharply with one of his shins, and he shook her again.

"You should have let me win." His tone was harsh, the words tumbling out in a frenzied stream. "If you had only let me win, you would have been mine and we would have been happy. But now ... when I take the crown, I'm going to go to your world and get a thousand of you. I'll bring them here and they will serve me, and when they've lived their short insignificant lives, I shall get a thousand more and a thousand more and it will all be your fault. Your fault. Traitor. *Traitor.*"

His words, cruel and terrible, made her blanch, sick to her stomach. And suddenly she felt something bloom from her, as though she were expelling a live thing from her body, from her very flesh, an invisible thing that rippled and stretched and forced itself between them. Cole's fingers slid from her hair and he muttered an expletive, reaching forward to grab her again, but now his feet were sliding back on the floorboards as though he were being pushed back by an invisible hand.

She didn't stop to wonder. She merely turned and ran, the guide bobbing ahead merrily, as if it had no idea of the danger they were in.

The light turned down a hallway and into another and then she was in the forest again, but there was no safety there. It was a common area, where anyone might go. The only safety she had in the castle was her room, and perhaps not even there. She should try to find the Adjudicator, but no, that thought died as soon as she had thought it. She rounded the columns and cried out in shock as she barrelled into a tall, imposing figure.

"Ember," Ashe said, his gaze immediately going behind her to see what she was running from.

"Please." She clutched at him, her nerves so twisted and jangled she felt as if she might scream. "Please help me."

He gathered her into his arms and darkness enfolded them both.

# CHAPTER 26

The darkness receded, but still Ember clung to Ashe, and it was a moment or two before she could gather the strength to pull away, and mumble, "Thank you."

His eyes roamed over her, concern etched on his face. "Are you sure you're alright? You're whiter than bone."

"Your cousin waylaid me." An involuntary shudder went down her spine.

The muscle in his jaw flickered, the only betrayal of his composure.

"I took a wrong turn. He was practising his swordplay, and then he saw me and …"

"Did he lay hands on you?" His eyes glittered, his bearing rigid with tension. He looked as though he were about to bare his teeth in a snarl.

"Not really." Ember was unwilling to tell him the truth. It was she who had wandered into Cole's territory, she who had provoked him, she who had caused all the trouble right from the start—she suddenly caught herself and bit her lip. She could almost hear her therapist remonstrating with her. *Not* her fault. "He said that if he won, he was going to kidnap human women and enslave them."

Ashe let out a short bark of laughter at that, which reassured her.

153

"So he can't do it?"

"It would take far more power than what he has now. It would take more than what he would have as Sword, *if* he won the crown."

"But he took me once," she reminded him.

"With my help. And it was an accident. I'm still not entirely sure how we managed it at all."

He took a sudden indrawn breath, his thumb swiping her chin and coming away bloody.

"Not mine," she assured him. "Although I'm pretty sure it would be if the Blade hadn't protected me again."

She gently touched the pendant around her neck, but even as she felt the facets of the orange jewel under her fingertips, she recalled the absence of its warming glow, the lack of burning that had marked the last time it had thrust Cole away. This time, the barrier that had come between them was different, as though it had come from somewhere else. Perhaps the guide conjured it, she thought. It had always seemed like a friend of sorts, rather like a computer assistant with their friendly voices and eagerness to give weather reports and errand reminders. Maybe it was on her side, too.

"You're safe here." As if by reflex, he drew her to him, his arms tightening around her. For an instant, she rested her cheek against his broad chest, and she thought she felt the brush of his lips against her hair. Hastily, she pulled away. He'd told her he didn't want her, and for good reason, too. For a moment they stood, staring at each other, the confusion in Ashe's eyes mirroring her own, and then she looked away.

For the first time, she became aware of her surroundings, and with a jolt of shock, realised they weren't alone. The room was sunlit, pale wooden floorboards covered with a multicoloured rug in a complicated geometric pattern. Bookshelves lined the walls, and in the corner stood a trio of beautiful, lithe fae, two with stringed instruments dangling from their fingers, heads bowed.

A door opened and in bustled a portly fae with black and white wings. His whole demeanour was rather reminiscent of a magpie. "Come, ladies, let us hear you," he said impatiently.

The musicians lifted their heads at once. They raised their instruments to play, and the third sang a soft melody in accompaniment.

He then addressed Ashe, ignoring Ember completely. "Your Highness, I've asked Trebin to fit you for the ball. Is there any chance of getting you out of this," and here he waved a disparaging hand in Ashe's general direction, "and into a colour that's a little more ... colour?"

Ember pressed her lips together to prevent a chuckle.

Far from looking amused, Ashe was scowling. "Ember, this is my assistant, Caras."

"Yes, yes, I know who you are, young lady." Caras bowed, quick and deep, like a marionette who had fallen and then been jerked upright again. "Don't you agree the prince would suit a royal blue? Or a deep green? Or any of the jewel colours, really ..." His voice trailed off as he took in Ember's black military-style outfit and gave a weary sigh. "I suppose not."

"Caras, what ball? Nobody's said anything about a ball," Ashe said.

Cara's face blanched with dismay. "Your Highness, really. The Adjudicator will have his contest, naturally there will be a ball to go with it. I think we can do a little better than last time. I hate to say it, but the word *funereal* comes to mind."

"Caras," Ashe interrupted, his tone warning. "Find someone else to harangue."

"At once, your Highness," said Caras, bowing and backing toward the door. "But would you prefer blue or green, if you had a choice?"

"Out," Ashe shouted, and Caras shot through the doorway.

Ember couldn't prevent the laugh this time, and Ashe gave her an impatient look. "He's been with me forever, and his impertinence grows every year."

She crossed to the window and looked out, wondering in which part of the castle Ashe's rooms lay. The view outside was of a peaceful meadow. A black-winged mare grazed under the trees at the far end, and two foals played by the rails, both a dark charcoal with wings incongruously a translucent pink, like the inner of a shell glowing in the sunlight. They cavorted and pranced, their wings hardly strong enough to keep them aloft for more than a few seconds before they landed on the grass in a clumsy tangle of hooves.

"Oh, aren't they sweet!" Ember cried. "Why are their wings pink? Did they have a red father?"

Ashe smiled. "No. All horses' wings are pink at that age, and then they'll darken to their regular colour as they grow."

"Can we go and see them?"

"Certainly, if you wish it."

They left the room, but the music didn't abate. Reminded of the guards who had waited for her on the riverbanks all day in the sunshine, Ember wondered if the musicians would eventually fall silent and go about their business, or whether they would continue singing to the empty silence, like a radio that hadn't been switched off.

They moved through airy corridors, and the fae they passed bowed respectfully, although, Ember noticed, they didn't avert their faces and scuttle out of the way of Ashe as they would if he were Cole.

They went through a gallery hung with paintings, and Ember ran ahead to inspect them. Like all fae art, they were derivative of earthly works, but with tweaks that betrayed them: oddly shaded colours, figures that moved within their frames, fae with wings, horns and tails, strange beasts out of mythical fairytales. Unlike those hanging in Cole's gallery of horrors, these paintings were warm and strangely beautiful. And then she gave a surprised cry as she recognised one painting, an abstract of white bleeding into blue. It hung on its own at the far end, illuminated by a shaft of light that appeared sourced from nowhere, a bench positioned in front of it as if to encourage contemplation. She had painted it the day he'd whisked her away to a tropical beach, where she'd spent the most relaxing afternoon of her time in the kingdom.

"You kept it," she said with delight.

He nodded, ducking his head, and in that moment, he looked quite bashful. A wave of tenderness came over her at that unguarded moment, which was followed swiftly by a disconcerting melting in the pit of her stomach, and a sudden heat between her legs. She let out a little gasp. The burst of desire had flared so quickly, and yet had it always been there, dormant and waiting for him?

His head jerked up, his eyes darkening, as though he had caught her out, as though he knew exactly what she was thinking. His gaze flickered to her lips and then down over her body, and she had a sudden urge to cross her arms in front of her breasts. For goodness' sake, she thought crossly, flustered by her own arousal. There wasn't a hot pool in sight. Aloud, she said, "The horses?"

He shook his head as if to clear it. "The horses."

He moved off quickly, and she went after him, pressing her hands to her cheeks, certain that she was blushing.

Guards on duty swung the outer door open. A gravel path wound around the side of the castle and into the fields. Ember and Ashe's footsteps crunched in tandem, but otherwise, there was silence between them until they reached the wooden fence.

The two foals saw them at once, crowding up against the rails to get close to the newcomers. Their mother nickered to them, but they ignored her. She took a couple of steps toward them, and then, apparently recognising Ashe, went back to grazing.

Ember stroked and patted them, and Ashe conjured a couple of apple slices, which they crunched down with evident enjoyment. Once the apples were gone, their attention vanished too, and when a couple of butterflies flew too close, the foals took to their heels, retreating to their mother's side.

Ember laughed. "They're adorable. Have you named them yet?"

"Their owners will have that pleasure," Ashe said. "They'll be awarded to fae who have served well."

"You mean, Caras?" She couldn't help a smile at the thought of the stout fae astride one of the tiny ponies, and Ashe laughed.

"No, not Caras. Members of the court, with children who might one day take part in a tournament for the next round of heirs."

Ember chewed her lip thoughtfully. She didn't really know much about court politics or how Ashe ran his part of the castle. Cole didn't have any advisors, just servants who did his bidding. While Cole was lord over everything, slow to reward and quick to punish, Ashe was more like a beleaguered civil servant and she wondered if the foreboding demeanour that had made him so unapproachable when she'd first met him, was nothing more than a habitual mask worn to keep others away.

They stood watching the horses for a little while longer, and a silence heavy with tension soon replaced the brief levity that the foals had brought. She glanced down at his hands resting on the rails, and a thought flew into her head, of those hands clasping her naked waist, parting her bare thighs, those fingers sliding inside her.

*Stop it*, she thought desperately, and he moved restlessly from one foot to another as though she'd spoken aloud. And still the silence continued, and she longed to break it, but she didn't know what to say, and just as she was about to blurt out something, anything, he cleared his throat and said, "What would you like to do? I could show you a little more around the gardens. Or the castle. Or —"

He broke off and looked down at her. Her heart was banging hard in her chest, her breathing fast and shallow. The heat that had flared earlier had returned tenfold, and there was a faint ringing in her ears, as if she were about to faint. She wanted him and she couldn't bear it. It was going to burn her up.

His face was unreadable, and then his eyes darkened, his lips parted, and he groaned under his breath. "Ember."

"Shut up," she told him, her hand sliding around his neck, pulling him in close. "Just don't say anything."

Their lips fused and she was swept away.

# CHAPTER 27

A she's arms slipped around Ember's waist, and she cried out with fright as the earth dropped away beneath her. A shadow fell across her, the shadow of wings that had suddenly erupted from his back, huge and imposing in iridescent shades of black, purple and green.

She clung to him, the kiss forgotten, feeling the muscles in his back flex and strain as they shot skyward. His face was intent as he looked down at her, and for an instant she saw the reflection of flames in his dark eyes, flickering red and orange, licking against dilated pupils.

She tore her gaze away, and the next instant wished she hadn't. They were so high up, the horses and castle looked like little toys.

"Ashe," she cried, and he laughed, his arms tightening around her, and all the while his powerful wings beat hard and strong, sending a flurry of musical wind around them.

She pressed her cheek against his chest, her eyes squeezed shut, half terrified, half exhilarated. She had no idea what he was up to, had no idea that he even had wings. He'd never shown them to her before. Cloud mist enveloped them, and still they went higher, her ears blocking with the pressure. Moisture clung to her clothes and skin, and she clung tighter, scared she'd lose her grip. They burst through the cloud cover, the puffy expanse lying below them, golden tinged cotton balls that stretched on and on. And then the massive beating of his wings paused, and they were hovering in perfect silence, far above the kingdom.

She looked up at him. He smiled.

And he let go.

She scrabbled for him, but her fingers couldn't quite hold on, and she fell. A scream was wrenched from her, a scream which strangely echoed back to her as though she were in a marble room, and to her shock, she bounced against thin air just above the clouds, her descent halted by nothing.

She lay there, trying to process what had just happened. A thin layer of something smooth and flexible lay beneath her, the air shimmering with a familiar glossiness. She was in a bubble, she realised, a bubble high above the earth, and over her like a dark avenging angel hung Ashe, his wings beating slowly as he descended to stand next to her.

She was on her feet in an instant and, without thinking, she balled up her fist and punched him in the face. "You bastard!"

He put his hand to his jaw and blinked, looking more startled than injured, and that annoyed her too. Her hand hurt like hell.

"You could have killed me!"

"No," he replied firmly. "I would not have done that."

"You could have warned me!"

"No. I wouldn't have done that either."

"Why not?"

He made a gesture that encompassed the clouds below and the kingdom below that. "They would have heard. They would have seen. Now they do not."

Her hands were on her hips, her chin jutting in stubborn anger. "Well, it wasn't very nice."

He looked at her and there was that hint of fire in his eyes again, a feral sort of look that sent a dark shiver through her. "No," he agreed. "It wasn't."

"I didn't know you had wings." She wondered if he could hear the little catch in her voice, if he could tell that the wanting was back with a vengeance, and liquid heat was flowing through her veins. The adrenaline of flying and then falling had transformed into something else, something elemental.

In response, his wings unfurled, spreading high above them. "All the heirs and rulers have them, even if we don't show them."

"Cole too?" She'd never seen his either.

His expression became closed, his eyes narrowing. "Don't speak of him. Not here. This is just for us."

She inhaled, exhaled, tried to calm her racing pulse. *Just for us.*

"Your wings are beautiful," she said, and then, because it was true, "you're beautiful."

He smiled and leaned forward. His mouth was just centimetres from her own. "You are."

She didn't have to make up the distance between them this time. His lips brushed hers, a mere whisper of a touch, and she wound her arms around him, opening her mouth and sliding her tongue against his, eager and hungry, but he didn't respond, wasn't matching her intensity. He was holding himself back, too gentle, too reserved, and it infuriated her. She wrenched away.

"Please don't tease me, Ashe."

"I don't want ..."

"You don't want me," she finished for him flatly, and pushed him away. "Fine."

He cut her off with a growl, his brows lowering, his wings flexing with a violent snap of air, and at once she felt afraid. He pulled her to him, hard fingers sliding through her hair, yanking her head back to expose her jaw. "Don't fucking interrupt."

He bent his head and bit her throat, and she gasped with pain and pleasure, an instant wetness blooming between her legs. One hand was still at her scalp, bending her back, keeping her essentially immobile.

"As I was saying, I don't want to hurt you, although ..."

He looked down over her body, appraising her, and smoothed his other hand over her breasts. Her clothing disintegrated under his touch, crumbling away as though it were dust. Underneath, she wore a hot pink lace bra, her only concession to Gelen's penchant for frills, and Ashe's breath hissed between his teeth. He pinched a nipple through the fabric, and she mewed softly, arching her back.

"Although?" she gasped.

"I know you like pain," he said, almost idly, as though they were merely chatting about the weather. He switched to the other nipple, rolling it between his fingers and then bending to suck, softly at first and then harder, drawing the lace-covered tip deep into his mouth. He let it pop out again and continued, "Your heart beats faster, and you ..." He slid a hand down to stroke her between her legs and she gasped. "You get hot. Wet."

She wound her arms around him, and when she inadvertently touched the part of his wing that connected to his back, he shivered, his breath exploding in a soft sigh. She tried to drag his mouth down to hers, but he resisted. "I told you not to interrupt."

"I'm not!" she protested, and he gave her a little shake.

"Stop. It."

Obediently, she fell still, and he bent his head to her breasts again, kissing her flesh through the lace, and biting her nipples until, unable to keep silent, she was crying out his name. Impatiently, he yanked at the material, tearing it. Her breasts bounced free, the air chilly against her slick skin. He lowered her down to the web of the bubble, the rest of her clothing shrivelling and collapsing into nothing, and it was as though she was lying on the clouds in the sunshine. He rose above her, his entire body hovering a few centimetres above her own. She could feel the heat from him, could smell his fae scent, and it drove her mad.

She arched up, trying to get some kind of skin contact, but he held her down with one hand, his wings beating slowly, mockingly. "I like to take my time. And it's only this one time."

She frowned, and he raised himself higher, a gust of air skittering between them, making her shiver.

"Just this once." His voice brooked no argument. "Or else not at all."

Just to tease him, she slid her hands down her body and then up over her breasts. His eyes darkened as she slipped a playful hand between her legs and slowly touched herself. She could feel the slick juice on her fingers. It felt good. And she liked him watching her. She knew what her little performance was doing to him. His cock was rigid, his breathing ragged. But he was holding back. He wouldn't move until she agreed. All at once, her own touch wasn't enough. She reached for him, almost panting with her longing. She would have promised anything, if only he would touch her. "Yes, yes."

"Say it."

"Just once."

He moved down, hands on her legs, thumbs pressing hard into her inner thighs, forcing them apart. He didn't need to. She would have opened herself to him willingly, but he was too focussed on what he wanted. He bent to her, licking her folds, fingers and tongue thrusting into her, flicking across her clit, sucking on her until she was arching and writhing, her hands in his hair. The maelstrom within her was building and building in a heated rush, the sunlit clouds churning about her as if to be a backdrop to her pleasure, and she cried out as she shattered.

He groaned as she came and when he lifted his head, he looked dazed and yet elated, as though she had satisfied something within him. And yet, not everything, for a slow mist was filling the bubble, the dark cloud of his desire.

Finally, his weight came down on her and she opened her legs wide. He didn't enter her immediately. Instead, he raised himself on his elbows and kissed her, not the soft, testing kisses of before, but hungry, demanding, urgent.

She could taste herself on his tongue and lips, and she moaned into his mouth, squirming beneath him, arching up to him. He pressed the tip of his cock inside her and she gasped with the width of it, tried to urge him in deeper.

"This is a bad idea." His voice was a soft purr, his pupils so dilated his eyes were fully black, dark holes leading to boundless pleasure. He edged forward, and she welcomed him with a sigh, enclosing him in her wet heat just a little more.

"No," she told him. "Nothing about this is bad."

She kissed his chest and bit his nipples, revelling in his groan of pleasure. She wound her legs around him, urging him closer.

"Just once." He was panting now, the muscles in his back twitching with restraint and she understood now that he'd been holding himself back from her, not just since their time in the clouds, but perhaps since the very first time they'd met, that all he'd ever wanted to do was this.

"Yes."

He thrust. Hard. She cried out and then she was matching him, stroke for stroke, urging him on faster and harder. The friction was building, and she couldn't even feel the bubble beneath her anymore. They were writhing, twisting in the air, fused together with the over-whelming power of their passion. His eyes were blazing into hers, his head fell back, and he cried out in a language that was strange to her, and yet she knew it was an endearment that might have meant he loved her. She bit his shoulder when her own release came in an explosive rush and clung to him as they fell through the clouds together.

# CHAPTER 28

S he stretched like a languorous cat on the skin of the bubble, revelling in the sunshine on her bare skin, and then there was a sensation of being enclosed and her eyes snapped open. She was dressed and Ashe was, too. The moment, that brief respite that had meant everything, was gone. Done. Finished.

His eyes were dark, not with desire, but with a shade of regret. His wings had vanished, and with their absence, she felt an absence within him, too. She made to touch his arm, and he shifted position out of her reach, almost casually, as though he hadn't noticed her reaching for him. She knew he had, though. Ashe noticed everything. The flippant rejection hurt. She had given herself to him, freely and gladly, without coercion and without the dark, twisted passion that Cole had conjured in her. Surely Ashe must know it was different between them.

She raised her chin defiantly. "Don't tell me you think that was a mistake."

"Not a mistake, exactly."

There was a flash of pity in his eyes, and it offended her.

"Well, hopefully it's out of your system now," she said, striving for a light tone. "You had me, I had you, and now we can go about our lives. One time only deal, remember?"

He nodded and looked away. "You know that humans and fae can't exist in harmony."

She gave an exaggerated sigh, fed up with hearing it. "Fire and water, addictive badness, I know, I know."

"I don't want to do to you what Cole did. And I don't want you to …" he broke off, but she filled in the unspoken sentence with words of her own, bitterness twisting her mouth.

"You don't want me to mess up your chances of becoming Sword."

"I don't want you to lose your mind," he corrected her, but she had noted the hesitation before he spoke. He gave her a rueful smile and rose in one fluid motion.

She got to her feet somewhat less fluidly, briskly wiping her hands on her thighs and then proffering a hand to shake. He gazed at it quizzically, and she dropped her hand, muttering, "Never mind."

"I'll send you back to your chamber."

"When will I …" she broke off. When will I see you again? How needy could she be? "Never mind," she repeated.

"Goodbye, Ember."

"Goodbye Ashe."

The gossamer bubble lurched, and she thrust out her arms for balance, stumbling on the bubble's surface. The thin membrane split and fractured and for a dizzying second, she felt as though she were falling into a dark chasm, and when she opened her eyes again, she was inside her room, alone.

She headed straight for the shower, suddenly unable to bear the scent of lovemaking on her skin, wanting nothing more than to wash away the afternoon in a foaming cascade of perfumed suds. But with every stroke of the loofah, an unexpected sadness overwhelmed her, until a tear eventually trickled down her cheek. She swiped at it, took a deep breath. Ashe was probably right. There had always been a potent frisson between them, but perhaps that was just the natural yearning of fae and human chemistry. Although she had to admit, she'd never had such a powerful attraction to any of the other male fae she'd met before—apart from Cole, of course—and come to think of it, none of them had shown the slightest bit of interest in her either.

She'd never seen Ashe with anyone else, and the thought of it gave her a bitter taste in her mouth, but she knew she had no right to be jealous. Sex was like a sport to them, to be enjoyed without guilt whenever and wherever they felt like it. They were base, instinctive, animal. The magnetism between her and Ashe was thrilling and wild, but there was no future in it. For one thing, the fae were so long lived. In a few short years she would be old and lined, and Ashe would still be young and beautiful. She could die at a hundred and he would still look exactly the same as he did today.

But the way she felt about him was vastly different to the feelings she'd had for Cole. Cole had aroused a desperate hunger, a carnal craving. When they were apart, she'd felt as though she'd been severed in two. Her mind had been a chaotic whirlpool, her senses twisted, her memories stolen, her will eroded. But with Ashe, she felt none of that. She just felt ... a little sad. Still, perhaps the more time she spent with him, the more his presence might work away on her, stealing pieces of her until she was just a shell of her former self. And he would feel the same way. He would send for her as soon as he could, unable to be without her. She would act like a drug upon him too, and he might yet become as obsessed as Cole. And if he did, would she mind? She wasn't sure. If he were human, she thought resentfully, or if she were fae, then none of this would be an issue. They could enjoy each other, openly and honestly.

All the thinking was giving her a headache. When she emerged from the bathroom, she found Gelen with a tray of food waiting. She took the tray to the window and dismissed him, telling him she was going to have an early night.

She ate without appetite, looking out over the courtyard. The usual evening bustle below was more subdued than it had been of late, the absence of the centaurs noticeably conspicuous.

And then she jumped, startled, as a voice echoed through the room, a voice that must have also reverberated throughout the castle and the grounds, for the servants in the courtyard at first flinched, and then, like Ember, clapped their hands to their ears. It was the Adjudicator, his habitual creaking whisper as resonant as a shout.

"The contest of Swords shall begin in seven days hence. A sword fight between the heirs to determine the crown."

# CHAPTER 29

Ember woke early the next morning with Gelen stifling a yawn as he waited with her breakfast tray, clearly resentful at her being up and about so prematurely. She ate quickly, telling Gelen she'd be painting for the whole day, and she'd call for him when she needed him. He cheered immediately, gleeful at essentially being given the day off, and departed. When she had dressed, taking particular care with her face and hair, she called for a guide.

The hallways were busy, with an atmosphere of anticipation and dread in the air. Courtiers and servants rushed here and there, preparing for the hordes of guests likely to descend on the castle to watch the contest and ultimate crowning. With such short notice, the visitors wouldn't number that of the last tournament when thousands had turned up, but there would still be many who wanted to see the crowning first-hand, if only to protect their own interests. With such commotion and bustle, no one was paying much attention to her at all, and her trip to the forest was largely devoid of overheard snarky remarks and sidelong looks.

Although she was determined to get to the Kingdom of Stones, she approached their column with hesitancy, looking up at it uneasily. The memory of that whirling travel through space and time had already given her a queasy stomach. She smoothed her fingers over the seam she knew was there, but it didn't glow at her touch, didn't welcome her in. The stone remained unbroken.

She had initially planned to ask Alena for help; the forest fae was easily capable of sending her to the Stones if she had a mind to. But Ember had decided she wanted to keep her trip to the Stones to herself for the time being. So instead, she took hold of the pendant, closed her eyes, and asked the Blade for help.

"Tana, please, open the door for me."

She waited for the Blade's signature warming glow under her fingertips, but there was nothing. She tried again, injecting a note of urgency into her tone and an extra 'please' for good measure, but the gem stayed resolutely cool.

She opened her eyes with a frown, deciding that perhaps she might need to call on Alena after all, and gasped. The seam of the doorway was a rectangle of fire. It blazed bright and then vanished, leaving a dark doorway in its place.

"Thank you," she whispered, and stepped quickly through before she could change her mind.

The darkness of the portal was much worse without Ashe. She hadn't realised how much his presence had steadied and helped her through. It had been bad enough with him at her side, but now she was alone, she truly felt she might die. Violent winds whipped past her, flinging her limbs about as though she were a puppet in a washing machine. Her bones were cracking, tendons stretching and snapping, eyeballs bulging out of their sockets, teeth loosening, blood boiling. She screamed, and the sound ripped away into nothing. As her lungs emptied, they compressed like a sponge being squeezed and she couldn't breathe, couldn't do anything to prevent being torn apart, atom by atom. There came a savage thrust in the small of her back, and she flew through the unseen barrier into the cold grey light of the Stones cave, crashing to the rocky floor with a helpless cry.

She lifted her head just long enough to spill the contents of her stomach, whimpering helplessly. It took a while before she found the strength to get on her knees and then stagger to her feet. She felt sore all over, but it was infinitely better than being in that hellish darkness.

The columns of the Seeds, Skies, Sands and Swords loomed over her, the crumbled pile of the Shields column just another rockfall dotted around the cavern. Still shaky, she took a few steps over the uneven ground, stumbling as her foot caught against the rock, sending it skittering away into the gloom.

And then a shadow flitted across the wall.

She halted at once. Hardly breathing, she squinted in the near darkness. She couldn't see anything untoward and she wondered uneasily if the trip through the void had done something peculiar to her eyes. But then came the unmistakable shuffle of skin scraping against stone. She sank to a crouch behind the Shields' rubble, wishing she'd had the foresight to send a message to Sten instead of doing what she now realised uneasily could be construed as an invasion of the kingdom. A guard on duty would have an arrow through her heart before she had time to declare herself.

"I come in peace!" she called, and then rolled her eyes. *I come in peace?*

In response came a low growl that sounded nothing like a guard. More like a dog, but much, much deeper, followed by clicking and rattling. The scraping noise was growing louder, and now came a clinking, jingling noise, and an unusual smell, a sharp, earthy smell like smouldering, wet leaves.

Taking a deep breath, she peeked between the fallen stones, and the breath froze in her lungs, which was immediately followed by a surge of adrenalin racing through her veins, urging her to immediate flight. It wasn't a guard. It was a *dragon.* And it wasn't a cute baby dragon wriggling in a basket. This one was massive. Double her height—triple her height. It couldn't have squeezed through the narrow tunnel that led to the outside, which meant that it had come from one of the cave's shadowy recesses, passages that led who-knew-where. All at once, she understood why there were no guards on duty. There was no need.

The dragon moved, remarkably light on its feet, considering its size. It tilted its head, and its nostrils flared as though scenting the air, and Ember silently cursed the perfume she'd squirted on her wrists that morning. The dragon slowly turned and stared right at her. She gave a squeak of alarm and shot back behind the stones, the stupid refrain *I come in peace, I come in peace* dancing merrily through her head.

A thud reverberated through the cave as all four feet landed as one, and then it was peering around the stones at her. The dull green eyes narrowed, and its mouth yawned wide. Flames billowed at the back of its throat an instant before it let out the most godawful screech she'd ever heard, and a sudden blast of fiery heat engulfed her.

She drew breath to scream, sucking the flames down inside of herself, convinced she'd see her clothes melting and dripping from her blackened, burned flesh, but to her surprise, nothing happened. She exhaled with a whimper and the flames vanished. Although she was trembling all over, she was in pretty much the same state as she had been before, even though all around her, the rocks were scorched black.

The dragon took a step back and then another, shaking its head in apparent confusion, and the merry jingling she'd heard earlier sounded again. A thin gold chain with a couple of dangling tags hung around its neck, as though it were a puppy with a collar.

Slowly, Ember rose, her knees still shaking. The dragon took another step back, retreating into the darkness, and then, with a contemptuous snort, it was gone.

She let out a shuddering sob, one hand reaching for her pendant, thankful beyond measure Tana had been there to protect her. And then came a voice, sharp and stern: "Who goes there?"

# CHAPTER 30

F ire flared, and for a heart-stopping instant she thought the dragon was speaking to her. But it was a guard holding a flaming torch in one hand and a spear in the other, another three guards right behind him, all hefting bows with their feather-tipped arrows pointed directly at her.

She held up her hands as she stepped out into the light, and the first cried, "Stop!"

"I'm Ember." Her voice was shaking. "Don't shoot. I've come to visit Sten. The king, I mean."

The bowmen didn't move, and the torchbearer said, "You'll have to do better than that."

"He said I could come and visit. I've come from the Kingdom of Swords."

Ember raised the pendant, letting it swing on its chain. Two bowmen exchanged glances and then one came forward, whispering in the torchbearer's ear. The torchbearer raised an eyebrow in disbelief. "If you don't mind, we'll just confirm that."

The bowmen shouldered their weapons, abruptly wheeling and marching out, leaving Ember and the torchbearer facing one another.

The silence wore on and on and eventually she said, "Maybe we should go outside? The dragon might come back."

He didn't reply, merely tamping his spear sharply on the rock, before tilting the sharp metal point toward her. Ember fell silent.

She waited for what felt like a long time, occasionally glancing with trepidation at the shadowed corners, her ears straining for the jingle of tags. Instead came the sound of marching feet, and then Apoli burst into the cave with a group of guards behind her, hands outstretched to take Ember's.

"Goodness! When they said you'd just arrived, I came at once—lower that spear, my dear, you'll put someone's eye out—won't you come up to the house? We never expected to see you so soon, and all alone too?" She rattled all of this off in one breath, pulling Ember into a warm embrace, giving the torchbearer a stern look, and then tucking Ember's hand into the crook of her elbow. "But no matter, you're always welcome," adding with a slightly disappointed air, "with or without the heir."

Ember gave a half shrug and a smile, a little overcome as always by Apoli's flow of enthusiastic chatter, and they emerged from the dark cave into a scene of dazzling white.

"The weather turned as soon as you left. No more night balls until it clears. But there's plenty to keep us amused indoors, thankfully."

Ember sucked in a breath of cool air with pleasure, chasing away the last remnants of dragon fire from her lungs, and almost immediately shivered. The wind was bitter.

One guard shrugged off his heavy fleece coat and handed it to her—with some unnecessary flexing of his biceps in front of

Apoli—and Apoli gave a breathless giggle and remarked, "Oh my. Aren't you the lucky one?"

Ember wasn't sure how lucky she was, for the coat still had the raw smell of the farm lingering in its fibres, but she had to admit, it was warm.

The pass, although gloomy and dark, kept them clear from the biting wind, but the frozen moat was another matter entirely. Drifts of snow rose high on either side of the path, and the wind whistling through the rocky peaks and across the ice became a dull cry that sounded as though it were alive.

"Dragonsong," called Apoli over the clamour. "It strikes fear into the hearts of the brave, and adventure into the souls of the foolish. The villagers will have to chain their doors shut tonight, else there'll be would-be heroes marching into the hills and nothing but corpses coming home again."

And with that cheery snippet of information, they continued on.

Finally, they came to the palace. Ember slipped off the guard's coat, handing it back to him with thanks, which he acknowledged with a surprised bow. Apoli left her in the care of a servant and sashayed off, mumbling something about being late for a meeting, but Ember had seen the way she'd smiled up at the guard, giving a fairly good indication of what that 'meeting' would entail.

Once in a warm sitting room in front of a roaring fire, a servant brought a tray of refreshments, rather hearty fare compared with that of the Swords': steaming slices of meat, crispy potatoes on toothpicks, a mug of thick vegetable soup, and bread. Having eaten not long before, Ember opted for the mug of cider that came with it instead, sipping it quickly and letting the fiery spirits warm her through. While she waited, she leaned against the window, noting the colours and shadows of the mountain peaks, and wondering how best to replicate them for her mural. Snow fell, softly at first and then thicker, until it was whirling past the window in great gusts, obscuring the view altogether.

The door opened and in came Sten, surprised, but disguising it well with an effusive welcome and a kiss on each cheek.

"Ember! I almost laid dragon eggs when they told me you'd arrived! My dear, you should have sent us a message. It's not really done to just — turn up. You could have been killed, and then where would we be? Murdering the caretaker of the Swords? I shudder to think what the Adjudicator would make of that."

"I'm sorry," Ember said. "I didn't even think about that. It just seemed like a good time to come. The contest is in a week—a sword fight between the heirs."

"A fight to the death!" Sten said with relish. "Just like the old days!"

"Well, near-death, I would imagine. Seeing as one of them has to be the Blade."

"Ah yes, of course, of course."

"Which is why I had to come and see you now. I might not get the chance afterwards."

Sten's expression grew distant as though he were concentrating, and then his expression cleared. "I've sent for the Stone mage who saw you at the ball. He'll be here presently. Is there any refreshment you'd like in the meantime?"

"No, thank you. I've developed a bit of a taste for this cider though," she admitted, and Sten smiled.

"Yes, it does that. Perhaps I should send a few barrels over to the Swords for their cellars? A gift of diplomacy. And later ..."

Ember realised immediately what he was getting at. A lifetime on Earth had taught her what a capitalist looked like. "And then if everyone likes it, you might start selling it, perhaps?"

Sten gave her a roguish wink. "Perhaps."

"I don't see why not. Trading will help strengthen your ties to the Swords, just in case ..." her voice trailed off, but Sten knew what she was getting at.

"In case the Seeds decide to move on the grasslands and bring us to war." Sten sighed. "Many of our centaurs have left already."

"So have ours."

She didn't mention Swirl. It hurt to think of him, tucking her rose into his hair and leaving without a backward glance. Besides, she wasn't sure how much of the Swords' business she should share with Sten. She didn't have anyone to guide her in such matters. She might inadvertently do or say something she might later come to regret.

Sten, as if sensing her reluctance to speak on, politely changed the subject, and they talked a little about the windows that Ember had painted on her chamber wall, which she could tell Sten found delightful, if a little odd.

Presently a servant entered, followed by the Stone mage. The servant made a hasty bow and bolted without being dismissed, clearly uncomfortable in the mage's presence. With Sten there, Ember felt no such unease, and scrutinised the mage closely. When she'd first seen him, she'd thought he looked like a rock with protuberances all over his face and body, but she saw now that it was an illusion of tattooing, the dark lines etched to look like the cracks of a rock formation and studded with tiny gems to highlight certain areas. It was his eyes that fascinated her the most. They were a dark brown with dancing orange specks that rose and fell, as if lava were being flung into the air by a restless mountain.

"I'll leave you," Sten said.

The mage shook his head. Without taking his eyes from Ember, he said, "No, stay, my king. I'm sure we will learn much."

He held out a hand, calloused and rough, for hers. He inspected her palm, and then bade her turn around, running a hand across her skull and back.

"A real human?" he said in wonder. "Forgive me, but I thought you'd be taller."

She couldn't help a chuckle at that. He was smiling too, his teeth perfectly white, and set with tiny diamonds that flashed in the light.

"I was wondering..."

"Yes?" he prompted.

"Can a human become a fae?"

The question had tumbled from her lips without thinking. She'd meant to ask if he could help protect her from Cole's wrath if he were to become Sword, if there was a way she could escape him and the Adjudicator forever. But it was Ashe at the forefront of her mind, and of the obstacle that was keeping them apart. If she were a fae, he would be free to be with her.

*But what if he didn't want to?* It was that nasty part of her mind that just wouldn't shut up. *What if he was just using that as an excuse?* She thrust the thought away, focused on the mage. "Is it possible?"

The mage thought for a moment, considering. "It would require a complete stripping down of your humanity. You would have to bleed yourself out, drop by painful drop, eradicating your thoughts, your emotions, your very soul, before letting us in. And even then, our essence might prove too wild, too violent, too powerful. You'd likely not survive."

The little hope flickering in her chest died. She shrugged lightly. "No matter. It was just a thought."

"Will you let me look into you?"

She remembered what Alena had said, about how a Stone mage could dismantle one's mind. She'd felt afraid then, but she didn't particularly care now. Let him see. It didn't matter.

He took both her hands this time, and she gazed into the firelights in his eyes, watched the rise and fall of molten lava. All at once, she felt as though she were falling backwards, down, down, tumbling back into a soft floor that felt deliciously comfortable, like a featherbed.

He went through her mind as if clever fingers were shuffling a deck of cards, but it didn't feel intrusive or overwhelming. She had the urge to show him something and so she pulled out a memory of her in class, working on the castle that formed the centrepiece of her class's exhibition, and she felt his approval, warm and sweet.

He was shuffling faster, going back and back, past her life with her abusive boyfriend Bruno, back through the foster families she'd lived with, back to school, back and back, and then she was in the car crash that had killed her parents and she was being lifted from the remains of a burned-out car, crying with the chill of the frosty air, back and back and …

Her mind reeled and then broke apart, reflections, thoughts, impressions, and emotions whizzing past her consciousness at incredible speeds. Her entire sense of self was on the verge of being lost, but through it all there was the grip of fingers on hers, and she held on tight, because that was all she had left.

Abruptly he withdrew from her, and if it weren't for his hands holding her steady, she would have fallen. She wasn't lying down after all. She was still upright, but her legs were trembling, and she was exhausted.

He ushered her to a seat. The whirling snow outside the window had ceased, shadows were lengthening, and candles had been lit. Sten dozed in a chair by the fire. She tried to speak, but her voice could only croak instead. The mage pressed a cup of water into her hand, and she drank gratefully.

"Did you like seeing my life?" She gave him a wan smile. "I don't think it would have been particularly interesting for you."

"On the contrary." His eyes were bright with sparks that rose and fell, rose and fell. "Tell me Ember, when you said you wanted to become fae, why?"

"I don't think I said that, exactly." She struggled to remember, her thoughts muddy and confused. "I just wanted to know if it was possible."

"I'm afraid the answer is no. You will never become fae."

She shrugged. He'd already told her as much. But he was still speaking.

"Because, my dear, you already are."

# CHAPTER 31

Ember blinked, not sure whether she had heard correctly. "What?"

The Stone mage smiled. "I can see it. It runs through you like a vein of gold. Your humanity is the bedrock through which it flows. But it's there. It's unmistakable."

There came a soft cough from the direction of the fireplace and Ember turned to see Sten awake, his face not so much surprised, as alight with satisfaction.

"I knew it. I knew there was something. Dragons don't take to everyone. I thought little Pengrine would have taken your fingers off when you first met him, but no."

"No," repeated Ember faintly, her mind whirling. She was *fae?*

The mage spoke. "Tell me ... who was your mother? Your father?"

"They died in an accident when I was small. Robert and Willow Bailey." Neither Sten nor the mage showed any sign of recognition at the names, and she continued, her voice hesitant. "They were didn't have much family. I stayed with dad's aunt after it happened, but there was no one else. No money either. I have a couple of pieces of jewellery from my mother. Nothing valuable."

"One of them must have been fae. Or part-fae."

"But ... it's not possible."

"I think she's a Stone," Sten said decidedly. "She has a Stone look about her. Those cheekbones. Like sharp flint. And the dragons like her well enough."

"There was one in the cave when I arrived," Ember said. "It didn't like me much at all. It blew a fireball at me."

Sten looked taken aback by that. "I suppose your Blade must have helped you. Not much one can do against dragon fire. Even if you're a Stone."

Ember nodded. "The Blade inside, Tana, casts barriers and things sometimes. He helped me. He protected me from Cole. And he got me through the column to here."

"Did he?" said the mage. "Or was it you?"

She blinked at that, thinking back to the pendant, glowing hot sometimes, remaining cold at other times. There had been the time she had seen through the glamour of the necklace that Cole placed around her neck, revealing it to be nothing but a leather collar to control her. Alena had said that humans usually couldn't unsee a glamour. She hadn't been wearing the pendant then. She said as much to the mage and told him how Alena had given her a brush so that she could create her own glamours.

"Alena knew," the mage said, with a diamond-studded smile. "Humans can't cast glamours, no matter how many tools they have. Their minds don't have the right properties."

"You think she already knew about me?"

"Alena's magic is entwined with the Swords' castle, stamped into the bricks, and forged into every iron bolt and nail. She would have suspected something as soon as you arrived under its roof."

Ember felt a sense of betrayal at that. Alena was supposed to be her friend. Surely she could have told Ember her suspicions? But just as quickly, the feeling subsided, to be replaced by a yawning tiredness. "I'm sorry. This is just too much to take in right now."

Sten got to his feet. "You're very welcome to stay. You could return in the morning."

"Thank you. I'd like that."

If truth be told, she didn't think she could walk to the front door of the palace, let alone get back to the columns. Her eyelids drooped, and she made a valiant effort to rouse herself as the mage bowed to Sten and said, "Farewell, Ember. We'll talk again."

Half-jokingly, she replied, "Goodbye. I'm sorry that I'm not so interesting now that I'm less human."

He merely nodded, not exactly refuting Ember's words, and left.

"Will you tell Ruby?" she asked Sten.

He nodded. "Of course. But it shan't go any further than that, not if you don't wish it."

"I think I'd like to tell Ashe and the Adjudicator myself. I don't know what it will mean for them, with the pendant and everything."

Sten smiled with a hint of malice. "I'd love to be there for that conversation." He raised a hand. The whisper of a snowy breeze caressed her skin, and then she was in the same bedroom she'd had the last time she'd been in the kingdom.

A maid curtsied. "There is a bath if you wish it, or some refreshment?" She kept her eyes on the ground, her head bowed, and her tone was vastly more respectful than that of Gelen's. He usually spoke to Ember as though he were doing her a favour rather than doing his job.

"I'd just like to sleep, please."

The maid brought her a silk robe and helped her out of her uniform, and without bothering to wash, Ember crawled under the warm furs. She could see the evening sun through a window, just dropping behind peaks outlined with golden rays. Just like the gold in me, she thought, and fell asleep.

# CHAPTER 32

Ember didn't dream that night, and she was grateful. Her time with the mage had felt like one long, disjointed dream of fragmented memory and jagged emotion. She'd had enough of dreaming.

The sky was a leaden grey, and assuming snow was on the way, she washed and dressed as soon as she'd eaten and asked the maid to escort her down to the exit. Once again, the fae ability to anticipate and prepare accordingly hadn't failed; she found Sten already waiting for her at the great front doors with a contingent of guards.

One guard stepped forward, proffering a cage covered with black velvet.

"A gift." Sten raised the edge of the cloth to reveal a red firebird inside. It hopped from perch to perch, eyeing Ember with a mischievous tilt of its pretty head. "A messenger. You may want to send us a note one day." He pointed out a leather bag hanging from the cage bars, filled with empty gold cylinders and tiny straps, and muttered under his breath—something which sounded suspiciously like, "rather than just turning up out of the blue" which Ember chose to ignore.

"Thank you!" she said. "She—he? Is lovely."

"He. All the messengers are male. The females won't do as they're told. Impossible to tame." He gave her a resounding kiss on each cheek, his voice drifting to her over the tramp of the guards' boots as they marched her away. "Farewell, Ember. We'll see you at the contest."

She kept her eyes on her feet, blind to the natural splendour of the icy wilderness around her, too consumed with all that the mage had told her. One of her parents had fae blood. One of her parents had likely lived in these very mountains. Alena had suspected. And yet, the Adjudicator hadn't? She wondered about that. She'd thought the Adjudicator was the most powerful fae in Esha. How could he have not known? And what would Cole and Ashe say when they found out?

Her thoughts went around and around, and it came as a shock when a guard laid a hand on her arm, and she realised they had already reached the dark maw of the cave. "Wait here, m'lady."

Two guards went ahead to check the cave, likely for the dragon that guarded it, but presently they returned, telling Ember it was safe to enter. They went with her, right to the Sword column, and watched as she stood in front of its smooth stone, the firebird cage in one hand.

The last time she'd gone through, she'd asked the Blade for help and was sure he had provided it, even though the pendant had remained cool and lifeless in her hand. Now she wasn't sure what to do. How did one call on power from within oneself?

She placed her free hand on the column and closed her eyes, a fervent wish on her lips, but the doorway remained closed and un-yielding. She glanced around at the faces of the impassive guards and clutched the pendant, muttering under her breath, "Tana, please open the door for me. I don't know how to do it myself."

But the door remained closed.

She cast a self-conscious glance at the guards, still patiently waiting. Failing was so much worse with an audience. "Would you perhaps wait outside?"

She wasn't sure if they'd take any notice of her seeing as she was just a visitor, but they did as she asked, wheeling about, and marching off through the little tunnel to the outdoors. Once alone, she grasped the pendant again and called on Tana—out loud this time, in case he had been sleeping or something—but the doorway remained closed. And as if in response to her voice, there came the distant scrape of what she now knew to be scales on stone, a breathy whisper cutting through the dark.

"Come on, please!" she begged. She may have survived a blast of dragon fire the first-time round, but she didn't stand a chance if the dragon had a fancy to gobble her up. She squeezed her eyes shut and with all the force of her being, she willed Tana to answer, the facets of the jewelled pendant cutting into her palm.

There came the vibration of slow, heavy footfalls, and a familiar growl cut through the gloom.

Her eyes popped open, and she swung about, trying to discern the beast amongst the shadows, but there was only darkness ... until she caught sight of the glow of fire, billowing red and orange at the back of an open throat. She spun back toward the column and kicked it.

"Come on, damn you!"

Light blazed behind the doorway seam and suddenly it was open. There was a furious roar, a blazing rush of heat and flames engulfed her, and then the whirling darkness took her instead.

Predictably, she threw up as soon as she landed in the forest.

She brushed her knees, panting, eyeing the pendant with a certain amount of wrath. "Thanks a lot."

A warmth cut through the breast of her uniform, just for an instant, before fading away. Just a reminder that the Blade was there, even if he couldn't be bothered helping her. Which meant it must have been her own fae power that had got her through the portal—although she had no idea how she'd done it.

It took a few minutes to find the firebird's cage which had rolled under some bushes. The cage bars were dented, and the bird had lost a few feathers and looked decidedly shell-shocked, but he was still alive, which was the main thing.

Gelen welcomed her back to her rooms with a bow, and Ember handed him the cage before closing the windows and drawing the curtains. At her suggestion, he reluctantly opened the cage door, and the bird flapped around, inspecting every inch of the room. Eventually he settled on her shoulder and nuzzled her cheek, which Ember found very endearing, because she was lonely. Deeply lonely. She missed her life back home, her classmates, and her work. And she wanted someone to talk to. Gelen was too prickly and haughty for her to really relate to, although she had tried. And Ashe ...

"Gelen," she said. "Would you fetch Ashe for me?"

She had to tell him what the Stone mage had said. Perhaps it might change his mind about their relationship. Half fragile was surely better than *all* fragile. And maybe he would know if she had any special powers—or any powers at all.

Gelen looked positively horrified at the notion and shook his head emphatically. "I can deliver a message to his servants," he explained slowly, as if she were a toddler. "But I cannot *fetch* the *heir*."

"Fine," she snapped and went to the desk to write a quick note, in no doubt that Gelen would read it as soon as he was gone. Once alone, she used the bathroom, standing in the sunshine under the shower of water gushing from the wall. It would be snowing in the Kingdom of Stones, she thought, and shivered under the warm water, relishing the feel of sunshine on her bare skin. The Swords definitely had better weather, she decided.

Afterwards, she took some time making up her face, not just for the beautifying effect, but for the armour, the confidence that lip gloss and black mascara always gave her. What was that magic called?

When she emerged from the bathroom, Ashe was standing by the window. For all that she'd been longing to see him, she was unnerved to see him there so soon and gave him a tentative smile, which he didn't return.

"Thank you for coming." The words came out stilted and formal, as if she were hosting a business function. "I just wanted to see you. See how you were. I heard about the contest—well, I suppose everyone did."

"I'm glad the Adjudicator has finally decided."

"How is your training?"

He shrugged. "We've fought against each other since we were children. We know exactly how each other moves, how each other thinks.

I know his weaknesses and his strengths, and he knows mine. We're evenly matched. It should be a good fight."

She wanted to ask if he thought he was going to win, but she didn't dare. She didn't want to jinx it.

"I wanted to tell you—" she began, but a swish of bright feathers distracted him. Quicker than thought, he shot out a hand, snatching the firebird mid-flight. "Be careful!"

Ashe opened his fist, and the firebird immediately took wing, heading for the safety of the candelabra hanging overhead. He hid amongst the diamonds, the reflection of red playing on the faceted gems the only sign he was there at all.

"It was a gift from Sten. I haven't named him yet." She took a breath and said lightly. "It's a funny thing, when I was with the Stones, they said—"

He cut her off abruptly, his tone low and even. "I'm sorry about that, Ember. Taking you to the Stones was a mistake. I can't afford to make mistakes."

"Yes, but—"

"I can't see you again. Our time together showed me that. You make me ..."

"I don't *make* you do anything," she cut in indignantly. If only she could!

"... weak," he finished flatly. "If I lose, I'll be the Blade and you'll never see me again. And if I win, I need a consort the people will accept. Either way, I must be strong for my kingdom."

"But Ashe, you don't understand—"

"Stop, Ember," and he looked almost disgusted with her. "I've said how it is to be, and that is all."

"You're not listening," she cried, wanting to take him by the shoulders and shake him. "Just shut up for one minute and let me—"

His brows came together in a scowl. "I'll forget you said that."

It was the glacial tone she'd hated when she'd first met him, the tone reminding her she was less a servant; she was only a human, while he was a prince and the heir to the kingdom. Perhaps she'd misunderstood when she thought he'd said he loved her. Perhaps he'd just been carried away by the moment. Perhaps he'd said nothing at all.

She took a deep breath, trying to quell her rising temper, and said, "Whatever. But if you'll just let me explain—"

"I came to wish you well. And to tell you that whether I'm the Sword or the Blade, I will do everything in my power to ensure you're safe. I'm sorry, Ember."

"No, wait —"

But it was too late. He raised a hand, and then he was gone, the swirling inrush of air that filled his empty space the only sign he'd been there at all.

She stood unmoving for a long moment, unsure whether she should cry, swear, or throw something. And eventually, she put her shoulders back, lifted her chin and said, "Well, fuck him then."

From the chandelier came a squawk of agreement.

# CHAPTER 33

The next day, as she was gilding the finishing golden touch to one of her painted mountains, Gelen bustled into her chamber with a pile of colourful dresses in his arms, dumping them onto the bed.

"No," he said, before Ember could even utter one word of protest. "The first ball of the contest—and the *only* ball, I might add—absolutely requires all guests to be looking their best and not ... whatever this is."

He gave Ember's black suit such a look of disgust that she would have laughed had she not felt so annoyed. "Tell me, have you ever met Ashe's servant, Caras?" she said drily.

Gelen ignored this, continuing, "It reflects on me, I hope you know. Turn up in that and I'll be the laughingstock of the servant's hall. And as for that winged rat of yours—" the firebird gave a defiant cheep and flipped up his tail feathers to show his tiny bottom, and Gelen curled his lip in distaste, "—it's unsanitary."

"Fine." Ember threw up her hands, wondering how it was she had ended up with such a bossy schoolmarm for a servant. "I don't care. Do your worst. Not that," she added as Gelen held up a bundle of marshmallow pink frothy layers that bore a remarkable resemblance to a kitsch toilet roll holder.

It took several dresses and much violent disagreement later before they finally decided on a shimmering dark blue gown, held at the back of her neck with silver buckles and falling to the floor in soft folds. It looked like a waterfall, the antithesis of swords forged in fire, and she wondered if Ashe would like it.

*Stop it.*

Gelen found a pair of matching high heels in the closet, with straps as thin as a strand of hair yet strong as steel, and a pair of sapphire earrings that were so long they brushed her shoulders.

She twirled in front of the mirror. She'd been wearing black so long, she'd almost forgotten what she looked like wearing colour, and the artist in her appreciated the way the blue brought out the pink in her cheeks and the sparkle in her eyes. Gelen appraised her with narrowed eyes, and when he finally gave a nod of approval, she let out an exaggerated sigh of relief.

"Thank goodness. That only took—what, three hours?"

"Take it off," he replied, shortly. "It'll get creased."

She rolled her eyes at that, but got back into her suit again, trying not to notice that it felt snug and claustrophobic after the light gown she'd worn.

She sent Gelen off to have a break—or rather, so she could have a break from him—and stood at the window, looking absentmindedly down into the courtyard. These beings, she thought, watching the servants and guards hurrying about below, these were her people. Was it from her mother's or her father's side? And how would she find out? She gnawed on a fingernail, and then whipped it out of her mouth, knowing full well that Gelen would have a fit if he had to repair bitten nails before the ball.

There came the sound of heavy marching feet, and her initial confused thought was that it was a horde of visitors descending upon the castle for the contest, although why they'd come through the back way was beyond her. However, it wasn't feet, but hooves, belonging to a team of centaurs. At first, she was excited to see them—for perhaps Swirl had returned, and the dispute over the grasslands was over before it had begun—which was swiftly followed by a dawning sense of horror.

The centaurs were thin and dirty, ribs clearly outlined beneath dull, rough hides, noble heads bowed. The *clank, clank* of manacles drifted up to her, jarring and hurtful, the heavy iron that cut into their legs revealing raw flesh beneath. All were squinting, as though they had just entered the light after a long time in the dark, and all looked utterly wretched.

Guards in heavy armour drove them past her window and out of sight, and tears came to her eyes. Never had she seen such an utterly heart-breaking sight. Her tears dried quickly though, to be replaced by a burning hatred toward the Adjudicator, for it would have been he who had ordered the centaurs imprisoned, and toward Cole for aligning with the Seeds and sending the kingdom to the brink of war.

"If Ashe doesn't win," she thought, clenching her fists so tightly that her nails dug painfully into her palms, "The kingdom is lost." And then she could count the minutes until she was dead, too.

On impulse, she sat at the desk and took out the tiny parchments Sten had given her. There wasn't a lot of room to write much of anything, but in tiny, cramped writing, she told Swirl of the contest without mentioning her fear of the outcome. She didn't talk about the centaurs she'd seen either; she didn't quite know how to say it. Instead, she finished, "I hope you're home safe; perhaps I'll return to mine too." Alive, she meant, and only by the grace of Ashe, for Cole would grind her bones to dust.

She rolled the scrap of paper into a roll, slid it into the little gold cylinder, and then tied it to the firebird's leg. It was a fiddly task made even more arduous by the firebird's unwillingness to have anything to do with it, shaking his leg obstinately, and pecking at her fingers.

Finally, she opened the window wide and said, "Please take this to Swirl in the grasslands."

The bird gave a grumpy squawk and shot out the window. He made a clumsy circle around the courtyard as if undecided in which direction to go, and then flapped off over the outer castle wall in a shower of sparks.

It suddenly occurred to Ember that the firebird might just head back to the mountains instead. Perhaps he was only a messenger between her and the Stones. How would he know where the grasslands were anyway, much less who Swirl was? She shut the window again, feeling a little foolish. She'd probably lost her pet forever.

She returned to her painting, tilting her head to one side as she studied the effect of the gold tipped peaks, forcing herself to focus on her work, and think of Ashe not at all.

# CHAPTER 34

The castle's size was more than adequate to house however many visiting fae wanted to stay inside its walls, although some opted to erect magnificent silk tents in the grounds, great billowing affairs big enough to shelter hundreds. Representatives from all six kingdoms of Esha were arriving daily, mostly those who occupied higher positions in their respective courts. There were noticeably fewer than at the tournament, and barely anyone from the Kingdom of Skies. Few desired to undertake the journey again so soon, and many were leery of what might happen after the heir was crowned. The rumour of the Seeds jostling for position to take over the Free Grasslands hadn't remained secret. It seemed everyone was talking about it behind cupped hands, and the Seeds themselves slunk around the castle with knowing little smiles playing on their lips.

During the last tournament, Ember had been the mistress of the heir and invited everywhere, to every dance, training practise, dinner and gathering. But now, as the catalyst for the second unprecedented contest, she was largely ignored. Behind her back however, she held the dubious honour of being the subject of vicious gossip and conjecture. Many fae felt Cole had been unfairly treated, that he should already wear the crown. Others argued the pendant would not have been won if someone unworthy couldn't take it. Some were even speculating that perhaps anyone might win the pendant, and she'd seen so many covetous glances at the jewel hanging around her neck, that she now wore it under her suit next to her skin, unwilling to have it yanked from her neck by someone thinking to take the kingdom for themselves.

She had only been invited to one party ahead of the ball, a simple gathering of the Stones in their marquee in a secluded corner of the grounds, and she was glad to be there.

"I told Ruby about you," Sten told her quietly, as they took their seats at a dining table laden with the best from the Swords' kitchens and several barbequed dishes cooked on the Stones' campfires encircling the tent. "And she agrees that you're one of us, especially after she heard you'd survived Nellie's wrath. Ruby thinks Nellie missed on purpose."

Ember spluttered. "That monster in the cave is called Nellie?"

"Not a monster," Sten said reprovingly. "A gracious lady who has gifted us many dragons over her lifetime."

"I apologise," she said demurely, although her eyes danced merrily. *Nellie?*

Sten still looked offended, and so she changed the subject to the firebird, telling him she'd sent the bird off on his first errand. "Do you think he went to the mountains instead?"

Sten shook his head. "He would do his best to comply with your request, even if he died in the attempt. The grasslands are far, far away. It might be weeks before you get a response."

"It wasn't even important," Ember said, rather stricken at the thought that the bird might sacrifice its life for such a banal message. "I just wanted to contact a friend."

Sten gave a rueful smile. "Centaurs have no friends in the Swords' kingdom anymore."

A pair of twinkling blue eyes were observing her from the far end of the table. It was the fae who had danced with her at the night ball, Kalin. He lifted his glass to her, and she tipped hers in return, smiling. After the table had been vanished away to make room for dancing, he sought her out and she spent a few happy hours twirling beneath the silken roof to the earthy beat of the Stones' musicians. Whenever she was with the Stones, she had fun. She was lucky to be one of them, she decided.

As they danced, Kalin whispered outrageous compliments in her ear that made her blush. He admired her, teased her, his eyes showing he clearly wanted more, but he didn't press. She returned to her room alone, pleasantly tipsy and happy, and the brooding figure in black hardly crossed her mind at all.

On the day of the ball itself, Gelen took charge of her toilette, supervising her bath and prepping every inch of her. He removed hair, rubbed in creams and lotions, daubed her skin with sparkling dust, and painted her face. He demanded she wear a headdress of towering fake curls to "cover that monstrosity of a cut" and only relented when Ember threatened to get back into her black suit and damn his reputation in the servants' hall altogether. Instead, she chose a headpiece of diamonds and dark blue flowers that gave her the air of a dangerous fairy. Gelen gave his grudging approval, although she did catch him glancing at the curly wig longingly when he thought she wasn't watching.

Finally, she was done, and both stared at her reflection in the mirror. She looked stunning, mysterious, imposing. She gave Gelen a quick peck on his cheek in thanks, which she could tell he was dying to rub off as soon as her back had turned. Once he had changed into his matching dark blue formalwear, he escorted her through the halls, reprimanding her for walking too quickly lest she sweat and ruin her dress.

The ballroom was dazzling with gold and precious gems, a display of wealth and power that let the visitors know in no uncertain terms which of Esha's kingdoms considered itself the mightiest. The sensual, pulsating music that she associated with the Swords filled the air, and servants moved through the throng, offering drinks and nibbles on gold trays. In the middle of the floor stood a platform, and behind it, the tree where the pendant had once lived. She felt the orange jewel twitch against her breastbone. It seemed Tana had recognised the tree too, although now it was bare of flames, its burned black branches like witch's fingers clawing up into the air, leaves withered and grey.

She saw Cole almost at once, his head flung back in a laugh, two gorgeous female fae flanking him. They were all dressed in the same cream, gold and shimmering sand tones, like a trio of palomino show ponies, a perfect contrast to the bright colours all around them. He caught her eye and winked at her. She quickly looked away, mortified to be caught staring at him, and flinched as she realised the Adjudicator was standing right next to her with his red-cloaked entourage of jurors, silent and unmoving like a cluster of rocks in a river as the fae dipped and whirled about them.

"My dear. You look lovely."

"Thank you," she replied.

He had an amused gleam in his eyes, which immediately aroused her suspicions. She was about to ask him if he was having a pleasant time, the reliable conversation starter of an introvert forced to small talk, when the Adjudicator snapped his fingers. At her startled glance, he pointed upward.

A cage was descending toward them, a golden cage like that belonging to her firebird, but large enough to hold a black leather chair and a side table. It landed with a soft thud, the door swung open, and the Adjudicator said, "For your protection, my dear. This is an official event. We can't have anything untoward derailing the ceremonies before the contest. Nothing shall be left to chance, and nothing shall be left to the vagaries of your human nature."

Ember gave a bark of startled laughter, which quickly died on her lips. "I'm not going in there."

He didn't bother replying, but there came a cold pressure at the back of her neck, like that of a powerful hand holding her. The grip was gentle at first and then squeezed harder and harder until she gasped and stumbled forward, sure that he was about to break her neck. The pendant jerked, and the pressure on her neck released, but by then she was already inside the cage, the door slamming shut behind her.

She clung to the bars as the cage lifted into the air. It rocked wildly, and she was sure the Adjudicator was doing it on purpose. He watched her with a smile on his thin lips and she had an uncontrollable urge to spit on him, but the glob turned into steam with the wink of one crepey-lidded eye, and she didn't even have the satisfaction of watching him wipe it away.

The cage eventually stilled, and a glass of wine and two dry biscuits appeared on the table. She plopped onto the chair, ignoring the biscuits but taking the wine, and fumed. This was nothing but a show, a tableau to demonstrate that although Ember may have caused all the trouble, the Adjudicator had her under control.

From her view high above, she could see all the guests. Sten and Ruby were ensconced in a little alcove with privacy curtains that could be drawn as one wished. Far from looking aggrieved on her behalf, they merely smiled and waved at her. She gave them a half-hearted wave in return, wondering if they imagined she'd actually chosen to be a parakeet for the evening. On one side of the floor, Cole was embracing the fae who'd come with him, and one of them had already discarded her top, her head flung back in pleasure as Cole nuzzled her breasts.

And for the first time, she saw Ashe. His servant Caras had once again failed to get him out of his habitual black, and he was looking straight at her, his expression unguarded. He was furious. She gave him a timid smile. He nodded back as though she'd sent him an unspoken message and strode across the room toward the Adjudicator.

She got to her feet, clutching the bars. Ashe could not remonstrate with the Adjudicator, not here, not in front of everyone. It would be too public, too much of a declaration. What would everyone think if he sided with the human who caused this mess in the first place? They'd think he'd colluded with her. They'd think he cheated.

But the Adjudicator was moving toward the tree, his entourage in tow, the fae falling back and bowing as he passed, a ship cutting through ice. He climbed onto the platform and raised his arms for silence, which was granted at once, as though someone had hit the mute button, and even Ashe halted in his tracks.

"Once again, we are here to celebrate the crowning of the Sword. The contest will be held at the Meeting of the Waters. Our caretaker shall replace the pendant, and the winner shall take it."

He waved his hand. There came a little whisper from the tree, the sizzle of a drop of water landing on hot coals. Leaves straightened from their curled, crumpled state, bright orange licked along their veins, and the tree burst into living fire again.

The crowd clapped and Ember did too, unable to take her eyes from it. It was beautiful, alien, disturbing. A glassy veil dropped from the ceiling to enclose the tree, a magical terrarium to protect the crowd from the heat of the fire, a heat which strangely had never bothered Ember at all.

The Adjudicator beckoned to one of his entourage. The juror climbed onto the platform and stood next to him, head bowed, red hood shadowing their face. All watched, curious. The entourage always travelled in a pack in the Adjudicator's wake. Nobody had ever seen one of them on their own.

The Adjudicator stepped in front of the fae, loosened the tie at their throat, and let the red robe fall away. Underneath stood a female fae with long golden hair hanging in soft waves. She wore a black gauzy dress that blazed with fiery sparkles in the light of the tree behind her, and she had a black collar around her neck. Ember gave a shudder of recognition. It was like the one Cole had once used on her.

The woman raised her head, shaking back her hair so all could see her face. The crowd gasped, and then there were murmurs and outraged shouts. The woman was beautiful, and somehow familiar.

She had a vicious scar down one side of her face and neck, and her eyes were wild, her gaze darting this way and that, her fists convulsively opening and closing in a manner that seemed strangely familiar. And even high in her cage, Ember could hear the crowd, she could hear what they were saying, and the word chilled her to the bone.

"Serafina, Serafina, Serafina."

# CHAPTER 35

C ole and Ashe stormed through the crowd from opposite sides of the hall. Cole was aghast, his face as pale as the clothing he wore, but Ashe ... Ember had never seen such an expression of misery and rage on his face. He was burning with it, as evidenced by the trail of black fog at his heels, which soon surrounded him like a malevolent cloud.

If the fae had quickly parted for the Adjudicator, they fairly threw themselves out of the way of the heirs. As she had seen the servants do, most turned their backs out of abject respect, although, Ember noted, such servility didn't extend to the visitors from the other kingdoms who still watched avidly.

The heirs reached the platform simultaneously. Ashe made to step onto the platform, but Serafina waved her hand, and he flew back as if he were a tissue in the wind. He recovered quickly, disappearing and reappearing on the platform in front of the Adjudicator and slamming up a black, opaque shield in between himself and Serafina. Ignoring her completely, he hissed, "What have you done?"

"I brought her back," the Adjudicator said. "She is mine now. Although she has changed from how you knew her."

"Serafina ..." Ashe said, and his voice was broken, as if his heart had been ripped from his chest.

"This is not my sister!" exclaimed Cole. "She is dead. Do not believe him, cousin. This is nothing but a ghoul, a sick pretence." He turned and shouted at the crowd. "Do not be fooled. Serafina is dead. I saw it myself. She took her life with her own hand."

"Yes," the Adjudicator agreed. "And yet, she is not very dead, don't you agree?"

"Even you cannot cheat death itself," said Ashe. "It's against every law."

"I can bend time. And as it turns out, I can bend death too."

"And why her?" shouted Ashe. "If you can bring anyone back from the dead, why her?"

A voice reminiscent of the gentle chiming of bells spoke. "Why not?"

Ashe fell silent, turning slowly toward her. The barrier between them shimmered like oil on water, and then abruptly vanished. Serafina seemed calmer now, but there was still the quality of a jungle cat about her, stealthy, sleek, and dangerous. Slowly, she descended the stairs, crossing to Cole and embracing him. After a moment, his arms came around her, but stiffly, reluctantly, as though he didn't want to touch her at all.

"My brother." She kissed him on the cheek, and he jerked back, turning to the Adjudicator.

"Am I still the heir?" he asked. "If she's back, am I the heir?"

"She is under my protection. She is mine," the Adjudicator replied lazily, which didn't really answer the question, Ember noted, but it seemed to satisfy Cole.

"Welcome back, then," he said to her, and moved back into the crowd, his partners in cream coming to him as swiftly as if he were the iron in the middle of a pair of magnets. He draped his arms carelessly about their waists and let them bear him away to one of the curtained alcoves. To the casual observer, he might have appeared flippant and unbothered, but Ember, who knew him better than most, could see how deeply shaken he was.

Ashe looked down at Serafina, his mouth twisted, his eyes pleading. "Is it really you?"

The light from the diamond chandeliers caressed her upturned face, and all at once, she looked angelic. She replied in that strange fae language that Ember thought she almost understood, a phrase which sounded like the one Ashe had once spoken to her, high above the clouds.

He walked down the stairs to Serafina, and she reached up to touch his cheek. He turned into her touch and closed his eyes as she moved closer to kiss him on the mouth. He kissed her back, a tender, poignant kiss that became deeper, more passionate, a kiss that seemed to last forever.

And Ember, watching every agonising moment, felt her heart crumble.

"How nice," the Adjudicator said genially, and raised a hand. The music began, a pulsing, driving beat urging everyone to dance, and so they did, slowly at first and then with abandon as they realised the show was over and the night was theirs to enjoy. Below the cage that held her prisoner, Ember watched Ashe and Serafina dance, his arms holding her close, their eyes locked, as though there was no one else in the room.

She slumped on her leather chair, not daring to drink any more wine in case she had the urge to go to the bathroom and couldn't. The fae below had no such compunction. They drank and danced and became more and more raucous. A fight broke out in one corner, a group was having sex in another, and soon some of the winged fae were flying up and knocking her cage under the pretence they were drunk and off balance.

"Fuck off!" she hissed at one fae who knocked her cage sideways, and he vanished with a cackle of mocking laughter. She held onto the bars, trying to keep her balance, wishing viciously that she had a firehose and could spray them all and put their precious tree out and see how they'd feel about *that,* when the cage gave a jerk, and then slowly dropped.

The Adjudicator and his hooded entourage were waiting for her below, and she wondered uneasily if he had brought all the jurors back from the dead, like Serafina, like zombies.

The cage door opened, and she emerged with her head held high, although her footing was a little unsteady, and she had a feeling the flowers in her headdress were askew.

"You may go to your room now," the Adjudicator said. "Your part here is done."

"But can't I stay just a little longer?" She hated the accidental pleading tone in her voice, like a child begging to stay up past her bedtime. She was a grown woman, for god's sake. She had the pendant. And besides, she wanted to see Ashe, to see what he and Serafina were doing together.

"Why?" The Adjudicator's clouded eyes were cold. "There is nothing for you here. This is not your place."

In an instant, Gelen was beside her. He bowed to the Adjudicator and nodded to her. "I'll escort you, my lady."

"Go," the Adjudicator said.

The last thing Ember wanted was to feel those icy fingers on the back of her neck, and so she turned on her heel and left.

Gelen didn't try to hide his displeasure at having to leave early. All the other servants were there with their masters and mistresses, and it was clear he felt left out. She asked him to bring her some cider and plenty of it, and when he was done, he might as well go back and enjoy himself. For one thing, she couldn't bear his hangdog expression, and for another ...

"You might do a favour for me while you're there? Keep an eye on the heir and Serafina? And tell me what happens between them?"

He gave a sly smile, his eyes lighting up, and she could tell he quite fancied the idea of being a spy, even if it was for a mere human. "Of course, my lady."

He left, and Ember proceeded to get slowly and thoroughly drunk, hoping that an excess of alcohol would make her forget the entire evening, but of course, it didn't.

# CHAPTER 36

Gelen woke her with a potion to ease her hangover and the unwelcome news that Ashe and Serafina had been in thrall with each other all night. Ember's only comfort was that Serafina had left with the Adjudicator at dawn, and Ashe had retired alone. None of the fae knew what to make of this turn of events. Most were inclined to think it was just the Adjudicator making mischief, trying to prove to all that even if he had to give away the power of the kingdom according to the treaty, he still held sway over the heirs.

She had expected to see a gleam of suppressed glee as Gelen told her this news, but to her surprise, he delivered his message with a measure of gravity and sympathy which she appreciated.

"What does my lady wish to do today?" he asked once she was dressed and done with her tray.

"Never mind me. Get your head down. You look like you're about to fall asleep."

Gelen bowed gratefully. "I'll attend you this evening. We need to talk about what you're going to wear to the contest."

She rolled her eyes. "Something with feathers to go with my bird-cage, I imagine."

He pressed his lips together as if to prevent a laugh and quickly headed for the door. As soon as he had departed, she called for a guide.

The hallways were conspicuously empty as she hurried to the forest, and the faint sound of distant music and laughter wafted through the air. With only one ball to celebrate the contest, it seemed everyone was still making the most of it.

As she entered the forest, the music transformed into the faint trill of birdsong in the canopy above, reminding her that the firebird might still be out there somewhere, winging his way to Swirl.

She found Alena's pool and sank onto the bank, dabbling her fingers in the water in greeting. But Alena didn't come. Ember gnawed on her fingernail as she waited, nervousness beginning to take hold. She needed to talk with Alena, needed to make sense of everything that had happened over the past few days, and she had no one else.

"Alena," she finally called, hoping that her summoning the fae wasn't being rude or presumptuous. There was no response, and she wondered if she should dunk her face under the water and call again, but the water soon rippled, and Alena stepped out, looking aggrieved.

"Goodness, child, it seems you're here more often than not. It makes for a dreadfully uncomfortable relationship."

"I haven't been here in days," Ember began indignantly. Alena narrowed her eyes, and Ember made an effort to school her tone. "I'm sorry. I just needed to talk with you."

"And so, you bellow for me like an old woman screaming for her lapdog. Is that considered good manners where you're from?" Her tone was caustic, but her eyes were alight with curiosity. Ember grinned. However cross she was, Alena couldn't hide the fact that she loved a good gossip.

"You told me to come and see you after I saw the Stone mage," Ember reminded her.

"Oh yes. He didn't crush you to gravel then?"

"No. I mean—it wasn't fun. But he saw that, well ... I'm part fae. He wasn't sure if it was my mother or my father, though."

Alena gave a self-satisfied crow. "I knew it. I could sense it. Of course, he'd be able to *see* it. Not that he's more powerful than me—" and here she looked irritated as if Ember had declared otherwise, "—oh no, he just has a different magic. Older. More elemental. Some might say primitive."

Ember ignored the little dig and pressed on. "What does that mean, exactly? Me being half?"

Alena tutted. "There's no such thing as *half*. If you have fae in your veins, then you are fae. Some fae will tell you just because you only have a drop, that you are less than they. They lie. You will need training. Most fae are trained from birth and don't have ... *humanity* blocking their talents. But you can see through glamours sometimes, can't you?"

Ember nodded.

"It would be interesting to find out exactly what you can do." She studied Ember closely. "There's something within you. Something unusual." She tilted her head, closed her eyes, and murmured something under her breath, before fixing Ember with a steady gaze again.

"How come the ..." Ember paused, looked around uneasily, and then mouthed, "—*Adjudicator*—couldn't tell?"

Alena made a little scoffing noise. "Because, like many men, he has no interest in anything that doesn't involve himself."

"Right. Well, that's another thing I wanted to talk to you about."

"Yes?"

"Serafina's back."

This news caused Alena's perfectly coiffed head to jerk back as though someone had slapped her. "Serafina? The heir previous?"

Ember nodded.

"Perhaps we should discuss this elsewhere."

Without preamble, she took Ember's arm in a firm grip and dragged her into the pool. Ember barely had time to take a breath before the water closed over her head. She struggled, but Alena ignored her, pulling her downward, swimming through water that was changing from light blue to black.

It wasn't long before Ember's lungs were in a torment. She had to take a breath, she had to. She tried to peel Alena's fingers back from her arm, but the fae's grip was like a vice. Spots were dancing in front of Ember's eyes; she was losing consciousness ... and then Alena dragged her up again, faster and faster, and Ember exploded out of the water and flew into the air. She slammed onto the bank and rolled, spluttering and coughing, sucking in as much air as she could.

When she had recovered, she dragged herself to a sitting position, wiping the water from her face. "Seriously!?" If Alena had been anyone else, Ember thought she might have punched her.

Alena didn't have a hair out of place; her gown shimmered softly in the dappled light. "Fastest way to travel."

Ember got to her feet, swearing under her breath, swiping at her wet clothing with little effect. Unlike Alena, she was drenched. But her outrage faded as she gazed around in wonder. They weren't in Alena's forest anymore. They were standing in a forest clearing by a river, the distant spires and turrets of the castle just visible beyond the trees.

"What are we doing here?"

"I wanted to see what you can do, in relative privacy." The bushes on the far side of the clearing rustled, and she turned. "Ah, here he is. This is Tasar. He is young, but very powerful."

A male fae emerged from the trees. His wings were a very pale yellow, almost translucent, like a stained-glass window with a black vein tracing, and he held them closely around him to avoid snagging them on the branches. He looked very familiar, although she was sure she'd never met him before.

"I'm Lily's brother," he said in response to her inquisitive look.

Ember drew in a sharp breath of dismay. "I'm so sorry. I loved Lily. She was very kind." She was reluctant to meet his eyes, for fear of seeing condemnation and anger that she had caused Lily's death, that she hadn't done enough to help his sister. But to her relief, she only saw understanding, and a shared sense of grief.

"She was." He bowed to Alena and said, "You called for me?"

"The girl has power within her. Perhaps you can help bring it out?"

"How come you need him?" Ember said, doubtfully. "Not that it's not lovely to meet you," she added hastily to Tasar, and turned back to Alena, "but can't you just ..."

Her voice trailed off. Alena looked mortally offended, the smooth skin on her face becoming rough and scaly, and Ember remembered with a thrill of shock that Alena's regal bearing had always been a disguise and that underneath she was something else.

"Of course," said Tasar smoothly, easing the awkward moment, and waved a hand.

The bushes rustled and swayed. With a grisly roar, a creature lurched out of the bushes. Folds of skin hung from its face and body, the snout and eyes oozing a viscous grey liquid. It looked like a giant plastic pig that had been flung into a fireplace. It gave a high-pitched squeal that made the hairs stand up on Ember's arms, and lumbered toward her.

"Go on then," said Alena. "Do something."

"Wait—what?" Ember cried. "What am I supposed to do?"

She fumbled at her belt for her dagger, but she'd left it back in her room. The pig thing lurched closer and closer, and now she could smell the stench coming off it, rank and sharp. She darted out of its way, and it turned and came for her again.

"Guys!" she yelled. "This isn't funny! Help me!"

But there was no help from the pair of fae who merely stood back and watched. Ember turned to face the pig thing again, clutching the pendant and hoping Tana would explode the beast into a thousand blubbery pieces, but he didn't.

She hurriedly sidestepped as the thing charged at her. It pivoted, faster this time, and with no other choice, she sprinted to a tree and started climbing. Up out of its reach, she hoisted herself onto a branch and looked down. Alena was doubled over in fits of laughter, and Tasar, in an attempt to be tactful, had covered his face with his wings, although his shoulders were shaking with mirth.

"Oh, shut up," Ember growled. "I have no wish to have *'murdered by zombie pig'* carved on my gravestone, not that you care ..."

Her voice faltered. The melted pig was snuffling at the tree trunk, and for an instant, it had wavered. She stared at it, willed it to waver again, and it did. Standing in its place was a dog. *Her* dog, the gift she'd had to send away for fear Cole would kill him, once a cute little puppy and now older, but still recognisable.

She tumbled down out of the tree and gathered the dog in her arms, tears in her eyes. "Rufus! Oh, my darling …"

Rufus wriggled with pleasure, wagging his tail and licking her face, and then he raced over to Tasar, sat at his feet and looked up at him adoringly.

"Well done," said Alena, with a hint of mockery. "Although next time, I hope climbing a tree won't have to be a prerequisite for unseeing a glamour."

"What d'you mean, *next* time?" said Ember, and then whirled as a massive slug-like thing, all goo and pus, slid from behind a tree and made for her.

She had the trick of it now, the flex of a strange muscle in her mind that had been relatively unused until now. It was weak, but she could feel it growing stronger. The slug flickered, and the glamour fell away to reveal a fawn, long legged and timid, who bounded away when Ember reached out a hand.

"Very good!" said Tasar. "You hardly hesitated."

"Not half as amusing, though," murmured Alena.

Tasar sent a couple more ghastly beasts that looked as though they belonged in some twisted nightmare rather than on the forest floor, creatures that hissed and howled, and dripped saliva between pointed teeth, and both times, Ember saw them for what they really were: a chicken and a racoon.

The third creature that erupted out of the bushes was a spider, easily two metres tall, eight eyes rolling, legs covered with sharp spikes. She flexed her mind muscle to see the spider as it really was, but it didn't waver. As it bore down on her, she suddenly had a sense of foreboding. This wasn't a glamoured spider at all. It was a real fucking spider, and it was about to eat her.

It skittered toward her, zig-zagging closer and closer, and now she could see the fangs in its mouth, the tiny quivering hairs all over its body. She froze, her mind screaming at her to run, and her body not listening at all.

"Get out of the way, you stupid girl," Alena shouted.

Alena's cry broke through Ember's inertia, and she turned to run, but almost immediately tripped on the rutted earth and slammed to the ground. She rolled on her back; the spider was almost on her. A terrified scream erupted from deep inside her, a primal, elemental cry of fear that escaped her lungs, and miraculously, became tangible. A hard, unyielding barrier materialised in front of her and the spider ran right into it, bouncing back. It tried again, tapping the barrier with its front legs and testing it, before throwing its whole body against it. It hissed and clicked, becoming more and more enraged. Ember hoisted herself up on her elbows, watching the spider in disbelief, just centimetres from her face. The barrier had the familiar glossy sheen of the bubbles that Ashe made, but hers was ragged and thin, and she wondered with a thrill of alarm how long it would hold.

Tasar shouted something, and the spider spun sideways, as though an invisible fist had punched it in the abdomen. It sent one last malevolent look at Ember, turned, and disappeared into the bushes.

The barrier dissolved and vanished, and Ember fell back on the ground, overwhelmed by a wave of relief and weariness.

"Was that you, or the Blade?" Alena's voice, usually so even and sarcastic, held a hint of controlled panic.

"Me. The Blade has been rather silent of late."

Tasar helped Ember to her feet, and she brushed herself off, pulled a twig from her hair.

"Your power has a knack for protection. How about you cast a glamour instead? Turn this into something else." Alena held out her hand. A rock sat on her palm, an ordinary grey rock.

Ember squinted at it and thought, "It's a flower, it's a flower," but the rock remained a rock.

"No matter," Alena said finally. "You still have your glamour brush?"

"Yes."

"Just use that."

Ember felt a little disappointed. Seeing through a glamour didn't seem as impressive as casting one herself. Another thought occurred to her. "Do you think I'll grow wings?"

Tasar and Alena exchanged glances and burst into laughter. Ember scowled. Clearly not. Eventually, their merriment died, and Alena announced she wanted to go back to the castle. She made to seize Ember and throw her into the river, but Ember backed away. She'd only just started to dry off.

"No thanks. I'll walk back."

Tasar offered to walk with her, and it was only after Alena had disappeared beneath the water that Ember realised they hadn't exchanged a single word about Serafina.

Tasar and Ember set off, with Rufus tagging at their heels.

"I'm glad I met you," she said. "I wanted to meet Lily's family."

"We were so proud when she got a job in the castle. She chafed at the farm. And then they cut her wings—"

"What did she do?" She knew Lily's wings had been cut for disobedience, but she'd never known the details.

"She stole food from the kitchens."

"That's terrible." Mutilated for a pilfered meal! It was such a minor infraction.

"Some of the servants, the dancers mostly, are only fed when they perform. Lily didn't like that."

Ember stopped short, suddenly feeling very cold. "What?"

Tasar shrugged. "The prince is very particular. He likes his dancers slender and compliant."

"Cole, you mean." She'd attended many of his entertainments and dinners, all with choreographed dances performed by skilled and silent fae. She'd never known that they were dancing for their very survival.

"When she flew home with your glamoured wings, we were happy for her, but very sad at the same time."

Ember felt a lump in her throat. "I understand."

They continued on until they came to a field with tall meadow flowers. The castle walls lay just beyond.

"I'll not go any further," said Tasar. "See if you can practise your glamours. You don't need a brush. Pretend your finger is the brush."

"I'll try. Thank you, Tasar."

"Goodbye, Ember."

# CHAPTER 37

The meadow flowers arched overhead, a vast bouquet of reds and purples and yellows dotted against the sky. Ember had to keep standing on tiptoe to ensure she was still heading in the right direction. Insects hummed busily, and occasionally she came across a swarm of little flower fairies, their iridescent lights almost invisible in the sunlight. She sniffed her sleeve and wrinkled her nose. It smelled of river gunge and sweat.

"... and why would I do that?"

A feminine voice drifted through the flowers. Ember spun about, unsure where the voice was coming from, and then as another more familiar voice spoke, sank to a crouch, her stomach fluttering anxiously.

"Because I asked you to." Cole's voice was playful, but ever so slightly wheedling. Ember hadn't heard him speak like that before.

"You already owe me. You're an heir because of me."

Ember let out a shaky breath. That sweet, tinkling voice could only belong to Serafina.

Cole gave an uncomfortable chuckle. "Should I say thank you?"

"Even after death, you're still exasperating. This little plan of yours won't work."

"And why not?"

"So you'd sacrifice yourself for me, as I did for you?"

"You didn't do it for me. You did it for yourself."

"Ashe said he would become the Blade, no matter the outcome. And when it came time for the first game, he went down on his knees with tears in his beautiful, lying eyes, and said he couldn't. He was weak."

"You couldn't be the Blade either," Cole pointed out. "You just swapped one confinement for another."

"He begged me to forgive him. I would rather have died."

"Well. Clearly."

There was a pause, and then, "My master may not approve."

"Does he need to know?"

"When did you become such a cunning little fox?"

The voices faded, and Ember was left alone, crouching in the dirt, wondering what fresh hell she'd stumbled into now. Cole and Serafina were brewing up some kind of trouble together, trouble which may put Ashe in danger. For all Serafina's fawning over Ashe at the ball, her tone when she'd spoken of him was malevolent. Vicious. But it wasn't as if Ember could warn him. He'd made it quite clear that she was to stay out of his way. Besides, she wasn't even sure what Cole and Serafina were talking about.

Cautiously she stood, rising to her tiptoes to see where they'd gone, but she couldn't see anything for the gently swaying flower heads all about her.

And then a hand shot through the flower stems and grabbed her.

She screamed, reflexively twisting and giving a sharp chop to the wrist, but the fingers still held her fast. "Let me go! None may harm me."

The stems parted and there they were, mirror images of each other, gorgeous, golden, and poisonous. Even the scar that ripped down Serafina's face, tracks of forked lightning, only served to make the rest of her look more beautiful.

Serafina still held her arm, sniffing Ember's hair in a rather disconcerting manner, but Cole kept his distance, a sneer on his face.

"What are you doing, grubbing about in the weeds?" he drawled.

"I could ask you the same thing." She tried to jerk out of Serafina's grasp, but it was impossible. The fae's fingers were claws, digging into her flesh.

Serafina's eyes were wide, her nostrils flared. "A human!" she cried, and there was hunger in her voice. "Her smell! How can you bear it? It's intoxicating. And horrible, all at the same time."

"It's an acquired taste," Cole said, and a nostalgic smile tugged at his lips. "But once you've had it ..."

Ember flushed to the roots of her hair. They could *smell* her? No one had told her that before. But of course, the heady smell of fae often seduced her senses. She should have guessed it worked the other way as well.

Abruptly, Serafina yanked her close and licked the side of her face. Ember recoiled with disgust, breaking free. She stumbled back, scrubbing at her cheek with her sleeve.

"Get away from me!" she spat, and as if in response, the pendant around her neck began to warm and become luminous. *Finally.* Both Serafina and Cole's eyes flicked to the glittering orange stone, and Cole edged back as if remembering the last time the Blade had blazed hot between them.

Serafina's eyes widened. A hint of red stirred in the green depths, the fire that the Adjudicator carried in his own. "You're delicious," she informed Ember, before turning back to Cole. "No wonder you're both infatuated with her. Honestly, I was a little jealous, but now I understand. You can't help it. It's animalistic. Primal."

"I've had my fill," said Cole. "I nearly choked with it."

"And now it's Ashe's turn," said Serafina complacently. "And then me."

"I'm not an apple you can pass around and nibble on," Ember hissed. "I'm under the protection of the Adjudicator. You all keep forgetting that."

The mere mention of her master provoked a look of fear and respect in Serafina's eyes. "Of course."

"Run off to Ashe, then," Cole said. "Go and tell tales. You two are a pair! Prince Unreliable and Mistress Betrayal."

"Is he who you want as your Sword?" Serafina asked. "You want Ashe to wear the crown?"

"Not my Sword," she reminded them. "As soon as the contest is done, I'm gone."

Cole stared at her, eyes unblinking, like a snake poised to strike. "And when I'm Sword, I'll find you."

A shiver went down her spine, but Tana was warm on her chest, and she was sick of sparring. She was beginning to get a headache, and it was like hot bands pressing around her skull. All she wanted to do was lie down. "Hardly. You'll be the Blade. You could try killing yourself too, but I doubt anyone will want to bring you back."

His lips drew back in a snarl, and he made to grab her, but Tana finally sprang into life. A bolt of fiery energy ripped from the pendant and exploded outward, sending all three of them flying.

Ember lay on her back for a few moments, blinking as the flower heads slowly came back into focus, and then struggled to sit, groaning under her breath. It was the second time that day she'd been hurled through the air, and her entire body was just one big ache. The surrounding flowers lay charred and smoking, and she was at the centre of it all, in the eye of a supernatural hurricane. Serafina and Cole had vanished, and when she could stand, she hobbled back to the castle, alone.

# CHAPTER 38

When Ember was safely back in her rooms, she went over and over the conversation she'd overheard between Serafina and Cole, but she couldn't make head nor tail of it. The only thing that was clear was that Ashe had promised Serafina he'd be the Blade—even if he won—but hadn't kept his promise. She wasn't sure how to feel about that. She couldn't even ask Ashe about it, for he expected her to keep her distance. And so, she tried to forget the whole thing, determined to spend her last days in the kingdom doing the things she enjoyed.

She ordered her favourite food and drinks, and painted quick canvases filled with colour and energy: the night ball, the baby dragons, the field of wildflowers, Riverburn, the temples.

The final canvas she painted was of the centaurs marching under her window, not in dirt and chains, but with armour and flags, stern and proud, ready to defend their homeland. On a whim, she picked up Alena's glamour brush, sliding the soft bristles across the flank of a centaur, and broke into a delighted chuckle as the creature stamped its little hoof. She quickly daubed all the centaurs she'd painted, and at once they sprang to life. In contrast to their military armour and

233

warlike expressions, they cavorted and galloped about as if they were young and enjoying a day in the sun.

She watched them with amusement, and then she had a thought. Slowly, she picked up the brush again and painted long strokes along her feet, up her legs, her torso and head. She didn't have to paint every inch. As if the brush knew what to do, her entire body slowly lost its colour and form until she was invisible.

She called for a guide, and when the little light appeared in the doorway, it bobbed about uncertainly, almost as though it were searching for the caller.

"I'm here!" she reassured it, and the guide became still. "Take me to the imprisoned centaurs."

It bobbed again as if nodding and shot off down the corridor.

"Slow down!" Ember called. No point being invisible if everyone could hear you huffing and puffing. It slowed down to let her catch up, and they continued on.

She had never visited the dungeons below the castle. There were no shiny waxed floors, diamond chandeliers or intricate silk hangings. These corridors were barely lit and mysterious shadows of who-knew-what crawled up the walls. Rough stone echoed underfoot, and grey lichen grew in dark cracks. A chill permeated the air, a miasma of despair and misery.

They passed a couple of guards who watched the guide curiously, but didn't attempt to stop the light or hinder it in any way. It must be boring down here for them, Ember thought as she tiptoed past, with nothing but silence and shadows for company.

The corridors twisted and turned, with stairways that appeared in dark niches. She had completely lost her sense of direction. If the guide disappeared, she'd be stuck down here forever, wandering around like a lost spirit.

Eventually, they came to a door set with an open window, and the guide paused, hovering patiently.

She peeped through the window, and there they were. Fifteen, twenty centaurs, lying on wisps of filthy straw, eyes closed, their breathing shallow. The rotting stench of infected wounds and bodily waste was sickening, and she had to take shallow breaths. All were wearing golden halters, the richness of their trappings at odds with their dirty cell, but as she looked closer, the gold flickered and became nothing but frayed brown rope. There was no lock on the door. It swung open at a touch, and she wondered at that. Any one of them could easily have escaped.

She instructed the guide to wait, and at the sound of her voice, heads came up—all those that could. Some of the centaurs could barely open their eyes.

"I'm a friend," Ember said in a low voice. "I'm going to get you out."

"Is thou a ghost or mischief-maker?" one centaur asked dreamily. His voice was hoarse, as if it had been unused for a long time.

"Uh ... a mischief-maker, I guess."

She stepped into the cell, being careful where she put her feet, and untied his halter. The effect on the centaur was immediate. He struggled to his feet, dazed and confused, and let out a soft whinny of consternation. "No grass? No sunlight? What is this place?"

With a sinking feeling of shock, Ember realised the halters hadn't just been glamoured. They'd been enchanted. The centaurs were in some kind of fever dream, enjoying a heavenly pasture of green, while their bodies wasted away.

"You're in a dungeon under the castle," she said, frantically untying one halter after another. "And it's time to go home."

The centaurs who were free almost went mad at that, shivering and stamping, and Ember flew to the door to check a guard hadn't heard.

"Shut up, please, or we're all going to get caught!" She willed the glamour to fall away, and as she appeared in front of them, they fell silent at once. They certainly recognised the pendant around her neck, even if her face was unfamiliar.

Quickly, she undid the last of the halters. Some of the centaurs were so weak they could barely stand, and she had to urge them to their feet. When all were ready, she said to the guide, "Find us a quick way out of the castle, would you?"

The guide led them on a different way than that which she had come, a way which led further down into the bowels of the castle, and she wondered if it understood they had to get out *now*. She repeated her instructions again, but it didn't falter or change direction, and she had to trust it knew the way. At least there were no guards around, and she was grateful. The resonant clopping of hooves seemed to fill the stone tunnels, and she found herself frequently glancing back over her shoulder, certain someone would hear. The only light came from the guide and the occasional candle, and she started at the shadows, fearful someone or something was looming out of the dark.

The tunnel led to a door, and beyond that, a sloping dirt walled passage. The centaurs struggled valiantly up the incline, but some still had to stop and rest occasionally, Ember shifting from foot to foot with impatience as they caught their breath. Eventually, they came out under an archway into an overgrown part of the grounds. In the light, they looked even more wretched, and she wished she had thought to bring some medicine or balm for their wounds.

The slow trickle of a small stream attracted their attention and soon they were drinking, washing their cuts and lesions, and nibbling on fresh foliage.

The centaur she'd first released came forward. Although he was thin with weeping sores all over his body, his eyes were alert, his head held high. He took her hand and squeezed it. "How can we thank you?"

"Your people have gone to the grasslands," Ember said. "Can you find your way from here?"

"Of course."

"Then tell Swirl that Ember says hi."

An expression of confusion filled his brown eyes, but he nodded, and soon the herd was ambling through the trees and out of sight.

# CHAPTER 39

The contest to decide the kingdom would take place at the Meeting of the Waters, a natural basin formed by the joining of two rivers long ago. The water had since been drained and diverted to irrigate the surrounding farms, but the dip in the land remained, the slopes reconstructed with terraces and viewing platforms.

Gelen bustled into Ember's room at first light, but she was already up. She'd had a restless night, thinking about the upcoming contest, and couldn't eat a single bite of her breakfast. Gelen seemed pleased about this, mentioning offhandedly that the dress he'd chosen for her didn't work with a bloated stomach anyway. If it were an ordinary day, Ember would have eaten the lot and called for seconds just to spite him, but it was her last day in the castle. She didn't want to fight.

Miserable, she stood mute and unmoving as Gelen pulled the dress over her head. It was sleek in the bodice but with wide skirts that diminished her waist to nothing. She ran a hand over the silk fabric, appreciating the two-way shimmer between white and black, depending on the light.

"It's diplomatic," Gelen answered shortly when Ember commented on it. "Black for Ashe, white for Cole. No need to show your
preference either way."

"Smart. I'm glad it isn't red."

"The Adjudicator will be gone as soon as the heir is crowned."
He didn't add, "thank goodness," but his relief was there, palpable,
hanging in the air between them. "No need to flatter him with pretty
colours."

He cinched in the wide sash with a heartless yank, and Ember
gasped. "D'you think you could let me breathe, at least?"

Gelen tutted under his breath but relented, loosening the sash
before tying it at the back. When he was done, she stepped in front of
the mirror and gave a half-hearted twirl. Her makeup and hair were
impeccable, but the black of the dress made her look as fragile as a
porcelain doll, accentuating the dark shadows under her eyes, and
when the fabric transformed to white, it gave her complexion a pasty
pallor, as though she had spent all summer indoors.

He handed her a matching lace parasol, and she looked at it doubtfully. "Really?"

"I think it would be best to shade your face," he said shortly, and
although she was a little offended by that, she had to agree he was
probably right. She couldn't afford to show favouritism either way.

He and a team of armoured guards escorted her through the castle, joining throngs of fae, both from the Kingdom of Swords, and
those from further afield. The excitement was infectious, but there
was trepidation too. None had forgotten Cole's murderous outburst
after the last tournament, and none had forgotten who had provoked
him into it. Ember kept her head down, ignoring the whispers and

sideways looks, and as soon as they reached the front doors, she put up her parasol, not so much to shade her face from the sun, but to shield her from their disapproval.

A long line of carriages met them outside. Gleaming horses and their drivers waited stoically as everyone clambered inside, white flags flying for Cole, and black for Ashe. Once the carriages were full, they set off.

Ember sat in a carriage with only Gelen for company, for which she was thankful. She was in no mood to make small talk. Her frock shifted from black to white as the carriage bumped and jostled along the coach path through the trees, making her feel a little seasick. She leaned against the window, blankly staring out the window at the gardens, trying to ignore her sweating palms and the dread feeling in the pit of her stomach. At least no one had made comment on the disappearance of the centaurs, and she suspected it was because their imprisonment was a secret. There were no centaurs locked anywhere, and therefore, there had been no daring escape. All was as it should be.

Although the Meeting of the Waters lay at the far end of the castle grounds, it seemed to take no time to arrive, and soon they were climbing out of the carriages and searching for a place to sit. The terraces along the basin were already crowded, and the atmosphere was forcibly festive. Servants wandered up and down with silver trays of drink and food. Musicians played bright, cheery tunes, and down on the basin floor was a troupe of tumbling acrobats performing for the crowd. Cole's white pavilion for the senior members of his court stood on one side of the riverbed, and on the other was Ashe's black pavilion. Once upon a time, she would have been in Cole's pavilion, clapping and cheering along with the rest. Today, she was glad to be just one of thousands in the terraces. Gelen led her down the aisle to the front row, close enough to see the sawdust scattered on the floor of the sword arena.

"Don't put me here," she said, horrified. "Can't I sit at the back?"

"The Adjudicator has requested you sit where he can keep an eye on you."

"I'm surprised he didn't put me in a cage then," she snapped. The memory of that night still stung.

"He wanted to," said Gelen. "But the heirs talked him out of it. Both felt that the caretaker deserved to attend like everyone else."

This slightly mollified Ember, but she was also sceptical. "*Both* the heirs?" Ashe, she could understand. He had hated seeing her in a cage last time. But Cole would have her chained and gagged if he could. Why on earth would he want her at the front?

She asked Gelen to get her a glass of Stone cider and then settled back to watch the acrobats. She hoped to distract herself, but her respite was brief. A hush fell over the crowd and all stood as the Adjudicator came down the steps with his entourage. The jurors were hooded as usual, none so much as glanced at her, and she couldn't tell which was Serafina.

The Adjudicator faced the crowd, raising a genial hand in greeting. Nobody cheered, nobody shouted. There was just a dreadful, gnawing silence, the disapproval of a crowd who had chafed under his thumb for far too long. Their lack of response seemed to have an effect on him. Perhaps he had been expecting some kind of acknowledgement. His thin mouth stretched into a bitter smile, and he turned back to the stage and sat.

As if they had heard a signal, Ashe and Cole emerged as one from their respective pavilions and walked down the dry riverbed to the sword arena. Both were bare-chested and wearing a loincloth. Ember wondered at that; surely armour would be the more sensible choice. But then she realised the point was for the battle to be decided quickly; one cut would likely be enough to determine the winner.

Formally, they bowed, and as the crowd burst into thunderous applause, drew their swords. Cole struck first, his white blade flashing in the sunlight. Ashe evaded him easily, and then lashed out with a combination that made Cole fall back. The two circled each other. Cole was smiling, but Ashe's face was grim and set. Neither took their eyes off each other, and then both struck simultaneously, their swords clashing with ringing blows that echoed across the terraces.

The fae were on their feet, urging the heirs on with roars of approval and encouragement, but Ember felt as though there was a large knot in her throat, keeping her mute. She clenched her fists in her lap and watched in anxious silence.

The battle went on and on. Ashe had been right when he'd said they were evenly matched. They circled, clashed, withdrew, circled again, and still neither had made the first cut.

Eventually though, it was Ashe who managed to slash Cole across the chest, a cut which oozed bright red at once, causing Cole to stumble as he fell back. He recovered quickly, and lunged forward, surprising Ashe with a vicious punch to his torso. Boos and jeers erupted amidst the wild cheers. Ember wasn't entirely sure whether a punch was within the rules, but the Adjudicator hadn't intervened. He merely sat, unmoving.

Winded, Ashe staggered back, before regaining his balance. An expression of absolute calm came over his face and his sword arm dropped as he closed his eyes. And in that moment, Cole followed up with a wild slash of his blade, slicing Ashe across the throat. A fountain of blood sprayed, drenching the sawdust underfoot. Ashe's hand went to his throat as if in disbelief, and he fell to his knees. The sword dropped from his hand.

The arena fell silent just as a cry burst from Ember's lips. She stifled it quickly before anyone noticed, her hand covering her open-mouthed horror.

Ashe fell face down on the ground. He tapped his fingers on the arena floor in surrender.

At once, Cole strode forward, a light of wild glee suffusing his entire being. He looked up, and his eyes met Ember's. He smiled at her, a smile of sickening triumph, and she realised why he'd wanted her there in the front row—to see him win, and to feel fear.

He laid a hand on the back of his cousin's scalp, releasing a white glowing mist that bathed Ashe's entire body. Watching Cole's power enveloping Ashe brought tears to her eyes, and she blinked them back before anyone could see.

Ashe pushed himself up to his elbows and then got to his feet, the wound across his throat visibly mending until his skin was as smooth and unlined as it had ever been.

Cole raised his hands to the crowd, and they cheered, a deafening baying approval that went on and on and on. Cole had won the contest. Cole was the ruler of the Swords.

# CHAPTER 40

Her ears rang with the tumult, and she wondered if the cheering would ever stop. The Adjudicator stood and raised his hands, but the noise continued. The jurors stood too, and a shimmer rose from them in a glossy golden sheen. It fell over the crowd, bathing the fae in yellow light, and making them all look a little jaundiced. A whispering wind grew louder and louder, the ground gave a jerk and just like that, the entire crowd was assembled in the hall with the flaming tree. The Adjudicator stood on the platform, flanked by both Cole and Ashe. The cheering in the enclosed space was so loud, Ember thought dazedly, that surely the windows might crack.

What tremendous power the Adjudicator must have to transport them all, a crowd of thousands, such a distance? As if hearing her thoughts, he turned and beckoned to her. Without volition, she found her feet obeying, step after step, the pendant rising from her chest, hovering in mid-air and leading her on to climb the steps.

She stood silently in front of the Adjudicator. She couldn't bear to look at the wildly triumphant Cole, and she didn't want to see Ashe either, so she kept her gaze on her feet. And then she heard Ashe's voice, as intimate as if he were whispering in her ear, "I'm sorry, Ember.

I was always destined to be the Blade. I know that now and I have made my choice. I shall take my place gladly, and I apologise for ever causing you pain."

She turned to him, and their eyes met. A thousand words lay in that look, but none came to her lips, and she hoped he would understand. There was a quiet dignity in his defeat that moved her deeply. Tears rolled down her face and, heedless of the crowd, she reached out and gently grasped his hand. His fingers curled around hers, just for a moment, and then he released her.

The Adjudicator gestured for her to take off the pendant, and she did so, pulling the heavy chain over her head. The orange gem swung back and forth, and the crowd fell silent. Golden rays came from it, shooting across the room, dazzling bright. At a gesture from the Adjudicator, she walked toward the tree. The Adjudicator had conjured a shield around her to protect her from the tree's fire, but she knew she didn't need it. She'd never needed it. Her own fae blood had protected her.

The twisted branches rose overhead, and the smell of fresh burning wood was overpowering, a nostalgic smell that reminded her of open fireplaces, toasted marshmallows, and cosy blankets.

She stood under the tree's flaming canopy and took one last look at the pendant.

"Goodbye, Tana," she whispered. "And thank you."

And she pushed the pendant back into its place in the knothole.

There came a flash of light so bright she fell back with a cry. Golden light spilled from the pendant, veining the tree in streaks of gold. Ember gaped at it in wonder, but only for a moment before Cole was shouldering her aside. He was eager, arrogant, already reaching for it.

Ember retreated hastily, having no desire to be anywhere near him, and then stopped, frowned. For a moment Cole had looked almost feminine, his commanding stride a dainty step of movement, his hair spilling down his back in a golden river. Ember blinked, and the momentary vision was gone as Cole plucked the stone from its resting place, holding it high before draping the chain around his neck. A shaft of light arrowed from the faceted jewel straight toward Ashe, striking him in the heart. He flung his head back and cried out, a desperate cry of torment and misery. And then he vanished.

It had all happened so quickly. One minute he was there and the next he was gone as if he had never been. Finally, Tana could rest in death. His replacement had arrived.

The crowd was in a fever of celebration, the cheers louder than ever. The Adjudicator produced a gleaming gold crown studded with orange and red jewels, the symbol of two crossed swords embossed on the front.

Ember felt a sharp tap on her shoulder. It was Gelen, his face anxious.

"Come, my lady," he said into her ear. "Before they realise they're allowed to kill you."

Together, they pushed through the crowd, forcing them to make way. The ceremony still held most of the fae transfixed, but others were leaving too: supporters of Ashe, and those from other kingdoms who disliked the outcome.

Suddenly, as if someone had flipped a switch, all was silent. The surge toward the doors halted. Time had stopped; the entire universe was holding its breath. Ember twisted around, craning her neck to get a look at what was happening. Cole was on the platform, the circlet of the Sword on his head.

And yet ... and yet ...

His features were flickering, melting like plastic in fire, and then he threw his long mane of golden hair back with a wild, high-pitched laugh that froze the blood in Ember's veins.

Cole hadn't been crowned at all. It was Serafina.

# CHAPTER 41

T he silent crowd found its voice and then came a familiar chant, softly at first and then louder and louder. "Serafina! Serafina!"

Ember was sure that the Adjudicator was unaware of what he'd done. As Serafina's glamour had faded, he had looked as shocked as anyone else. Now, however, he looked smug, complacent, as though he'd planned the whole thing. The tree blazed brighter and brighter, illuminating the avid faces in the crowd, and then came an explosion that rocked the hall. Many screamed and ran for the doors, pushing Ember and Gelen forward. The flames snuffed out, and the tree crumbled. A soft grey ash blew about in a little tornado for a moment before vanishing, as though it had never been there at all.

Ember and Gelen pushed through the doors and the departing crowd, dodging down an empty side passage. These halls were empty and there was no one to hinder them as they hastened to her room, hurrying as fast as Ember's tight sash would allow.

"It would be best if you wait in your room for the Adjudicator to take you home," Gelen said, panting. "You'll be safe there."

"How can Serafina be the Sword? How can that happen?"

"She was an heir. The pendant must still recognise her as such."

"Was that her fighting against Ashe?"

"I suppose so."

"But she's ..." Dead? Unhinged?

"The fair heir may have been unpredictable, but Serafina is ..." his voice trailed off, but Ember knew what he was going to say.

"Worse. She's worse."

"And she's under the power of the Adjudicator," Gelen reminded her, his voice bleak. "He still rules through her. It was probably his idea."

She didn't tell him about how she had overheard Cole and Serafina in the flower fields. Perhaps they'd kept their plan to themselves. Perhaps they'd asked the Adjudicator for permission to switch. It didn't really matter.

"And where is Cole now?"

Gelen shrugged. "Likely dead."

She wasn't so sure about that.

Her dismay and horror had crystallised into one driving thought. This was *wrong*. Ashe didn't deserve to be wielded by a woman who was clearly bonkers, with Cole likely planning to wreak havoc in the name of the Swords, while the Adjudicator took charge. The entire kingdom had been tricked.

When they arrived back at her rooms, she asked Gelen for a backpack, and then she tore off the black and white dress and got into her black uniform. She packed the bag with her meagre belongings, her glamour brush, the knife she'd bought at Riverburn, and a change of clothes. She told Gelen she'd go to Alena in the forest and ask her for help to get home. She had no wish to see the Adjudicator, and she wasn't even sure if he would keep his promise or just strike her dead anyway.

Alena would tell the Adjudicator she had sent Ember on her way. He would assume Alena meant back to Earth, and Alena would keep her secret. Cole wasn't dead. He would be demanding an audience with the Seeds, and she couldn't allow that. She couldn't allow Cole to bring about civil war and nor could she allow Serafina to rule over Ashe. Ember was going to the Kingdom of Stones to plan from there.

She was going home.

**TO BE CONTINUED ...**

# And Finally ...

Thank you for reading the second story set in the fairytale world of Esha! If you enjoyed it, please consider giving it a rating or review on your favourite book platform. For more info on all things Esha, visit https://www.tabithaday.com/

**Ember's adventure concludes in**
**'Destiny of the Sword'**
**Chronicles of Esha 3**

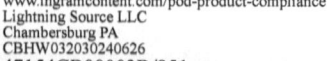